COURS & ENTRAÎNEMENT

1re GÉNÉRALE

NOUVEAU BAC

prépabac

Anglais monde contemporain

SPÉCIALITÉ

- **Aline Charles**
  Professeure agrégée d'anglais
  Lycée Descartes, Rabat (Maroc)
- **Anne-Cécile Couturier**
  Professeure certifiée d'anglais
  Université Paris-Saclay, Université d'Évry (91)
- **Jean-Marck Molignier**
  Professeur certifié d'anglais
  Lycée Saint-Michel de Picpus, Paris (75)
- **Christine Bitaillou**
  Professeure certifiée d'anglais
  Lycée Louis-Barthou à Pau (64)
- **Isabelle Kherbouche**
  Professeure certifiée d'anglais
  Lycée Louis-Barthou à Pau (64)

Hatier

Le site de vos révisions

L'achat de ce Prépabac vous permet de bénéficier d'un **ACCÈS GRATUIT*** à toutes les **ressources** d'annabac.com (fiches, quiz, sujets corrigés...) et à ses **parcours de révision** personnalisés.

Rendez-vous sur **www.annabac.com** dans la rubrique « J'ai acheté un ouvrage Hatier ou Foucher ».

* Selon les conditions précisées sur le site.

Maquette de principe : Frédéric Jély
Mise en pages : Nadine Aymard
Schémas : Domino
Cartographie : Philippe Valentin
Iconographie : Sophie Suberbère
Édition : Catherine de Bernis

ISBN 978-2-401-08675-3

AVANT-PROPOS

VOUS ÊTES EN PREMIÈRE générale, vous avez choisi la spécialité Anglais monde contemporain (AMC) et vous savez que la réussite dans cette matière demande un travail tout au long de l'année ? Alors ce Prépabac est pour vous !

Spécialement conçu pour vous accompagner dans vos apprentissages et vos révisions, il vous propose un **ensemble de ressources très complet** : des fiches de cours synthétiques et visuelles, des cartes mentales récapitulatives, des exercices progressifs, des sujets guidés pour vous préparer à l'épreuve finale du bac, et des corrigés détaillés.

Vous trouverez dans cet ouvrage **tous les outils nécessaires** pour mémoriser les connaissances clés sur les thématiques et les axes d'étude du programme, et pour acquérir progressivement les méthodes de la synthèse, de la traduction et de la présentation du dossier oral.

Nous vous recommandons de l'utiliser régulièrement, en fonction de vos besoins. Ainsi, vous pourrez aborder vos contrôles d'Anglais monde contemporain en toute sérénité et acquérir les compétences nécessaires en Terminale.

Bonnes révisions !

Les auteurs

Aline Charles

Anne-Cécile Couturier

Jean-Marck Molignier

Christine Bitaillou

Isabelle Kherbouche

SOMMAIRE

Les axes du programme

1 Producing and sharing knowledge

2 Science and techniques, promises and challenges

3 Every voice counts: representation and participation

4 Breaking the news and getting informed

5 Representing the world, representing oneself

Les épreuves du bac

6 Faire une synthèse de documents

SOMMAIRE

7 Améliorer son expression

8 Traduire ou transposer un texte

9 Réussir l'épreuve orale

1 Producing and sharing knowledge

Partly located in the Silicon Valley, Stanford University in California enrolls 17,250 students. It is one of the best and most prolific research universities in the world, with numerous grants and scholarships available for students.

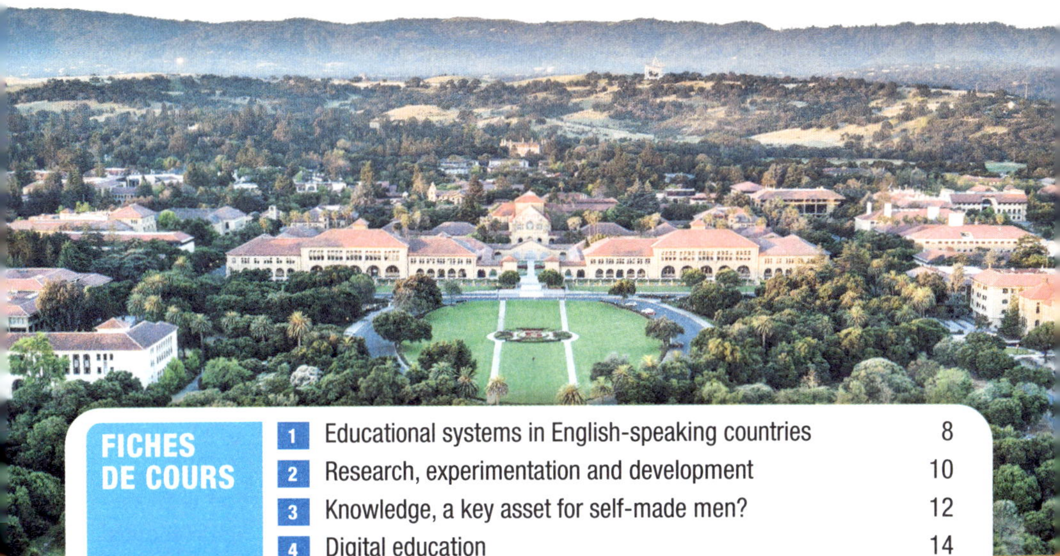

1 Educational systems in English-speaking countries

En bref *Studying in Los Angeles, in the suburbs of Manchester or New Delhi, may be a source of disparities. Students from different social backgrounds – boys or girls – are facing different systems and curricula. Is there educational equality amongst English-speaking countries?*

I Educational or schooling systems

1 Equal opportunities

- Common knowledge is shared amongst the different English-speaking countries. Indeed, the English language as well as the Anglo-Saxon heritage are to be found in their schooling systems.
- In most countries, there are two systems: a public and a private sector. About 85% of American children attend free state-funded public school, 11% attend private schools and 4% are homeschooled. In the UK, education is a devolved issue. Each country (England, Wales, Scotland and Northern Ireland) has its own system.

> **INFO**
> A **public school** in England and Wales is a fee-charging school, it is therefore not state-funded, so it is "private".

- Each country has its own curriculum and own historical narrative. However, a strong emphasis is placed on personal achievement in American schools, where pupils are required to practise sports and join clubs. Otherwise, it is a challenge for them to be accepted into higher education.

2 Educational divide

- In most English-speaking countries, education provided by the state is a human right. Primary education is compulsory, and secondary education should be accessible to every child, but is not mandatory like in India for example.
- Gender equality is not always respected. Girls' access to education is an everyday struggle for NGOs in India, while it should be a universal right (adopted by the UNO in 1948). Even if education is free, the cost of supplies can make it inaccessible, and parents prefer to send only their sons instead.

II Gaining knowledge

1 Access to education in the English-speaking world

- For the past few years, there have been new forms of learning, such as remote learning or learning with robots. Podcasts, augmented reality, voice commands (for impaired students for example) are more and more available. It also promotes upward mobility for those who are denied standard education.

- However, accessing these innovative approaches is a real challenge for disadvantaged and socially-excluded students. Social and racial divides in the USA make it difficult for some minority students to follow these new ways of learning and even if it is narrowing, there is still a digital gap: 78% of Whites, 67% of African Americans and Latinos nationwide use the Internet. More children drop out of high school in states with higher economic inequality (Missouri, Alabama, Kentucky...). → FICHE 4

2 Sharing knowledge

- There is more and more interaction between places of knowledge. Libraries, museums, and foundations have common programmes. University programmes "exchange" scientists, for example, for a set period of time. They can thus share their knowledge about a specific subject.

- However, a lot of individuals decide to leave their countries to work in another one in search of a better life and higher salaries. It is not really an exchange but what we call "human capital flight", which refers to highly-qualified individuals that emigrate or immigrate. If a country receives such an individual, it is called brain gain, while it is called **brain drain** for the sending country.

KEY FIGURE

Since 1953, around 26,000 Indian scientists have settled in the USA. This trend has been reversed somewhat – and is called **"reverse brain drain"**.

zoOm

India's education divide

- These pie graphs show the number of Indian girls and boys who are enrolled in higher education in 2014-2015. There are more boys than girls who are enrolled, with nearly 18 million against 15.4 million. Both sexes are overwhelmingly undergraduate (*étudiant·e·s de 1er cycle*).

- These data show that inequality between boys and girls is still poignant.

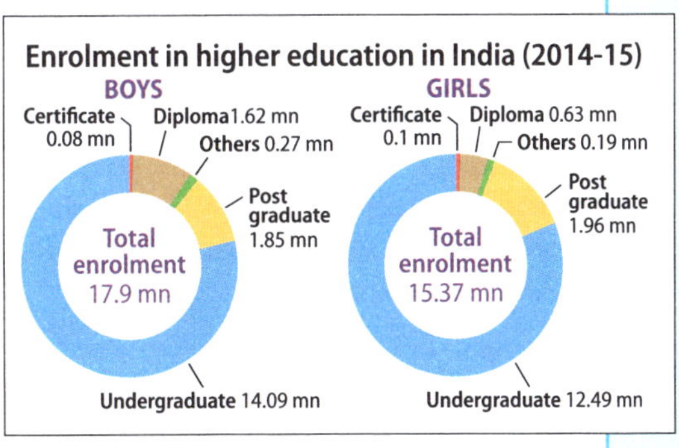

However, it is striking to note that girls are more numerous and outperform boys in postgraduate studies. They tend to have better grades than boys.

→ Read more about girls' education around the world: bit.ly/PbacAMC1re_1a

2 Research, experimentation and development

En bref *Research, experimentation and development are key components to providing a competitive advantage to businesses and nations. Universities are places of learning and experimenting while businesses contribute to financing that research. So how do universities and companies contribute to developing research in the English-speaking world?*

I University partnership

1 Universities as research and education centers

- Research universities are committed to research as their mission. Faculties carry out research which they can use as their course material. Universities in the English-speaking world are the leaders of research universities and dominate the **world ranking**.

> **INFO**
> This **ranking** includes Ivy League universities in the US such as Harvard, MIT, Princeton and Yale but also Oxford, Cambridge or University College London in the UK.

- Faculties who participate in research in their field of study are thus engaged in up-to-date data and can easily share that knowledge in their teaching.
- Research at the university level also encourages funding and investment to offer state-of-the-art facilities, labs, libraries, etc.

2 Circulation of students and knowledge

- Brain circulation concerns highly-skilled researchers' mobility, which enables the creation of a network worldwide. Universities have been developing their international mission statements in order to provide a better system of circulation of students and knowledge.
- For example, the Cambridge Africa programme promotes and supports African researchers. African students are welcomed at Cambridge, faculty members promote projects for sustainable development in African countries and scholarships are available. Cambridge has thus become a hub for interdisciplinary research, which mutually benefits the British university and universities across the African continent.

II Business plan for Research and Development (R & D)

1 Businesses investing in education

- For many years, big tech companies have pledged millions of dollars in education, providing discounts, equipping schools and universities and developing new tools. This merchandising of education and knowledge has accelerated with the Covid-19 pandemic, as students and teachers needed new and improved tools to cope with distant learning. → FICHE 4

■ Education has also become a field for investment. The GAFAM (Google, Apple, Facebook, Amazon, Microsoft) companies are motivated to invest in education for many purposes: it generates good revenue and students can use and get used to their products at an early age, increasing their **brand loyalty** rates.

INFO

Brand loyalty is when consumers show positive feelings and attachment to a specific brand. They would only buy products from one brand regardless of performance.

■ IBM also launched a free online platform in Africa called D-NA (Digital Nation Africa), contributing to Africa's innovation. This programme focuses on developing technological skills through free online classes. → FICHE 4

2 Business or government-based support in R & D?

■ Research and development are key components in promoting a country's power and innovation. The up-to-date data and research, the state-of-the-art facilities empower researchers and contribute to the economic, environmental and social development of the country.

■ While some countries' R & D is financed by businesses, others are government-led. In India, for instance, R & D is heavily financed by the government unlike the UK or Canada that favour business-led R & D. Public or private funding in R & D must be complementary as business-led incentives must be helped with public policies.

zoOm

DNA – Digitising Africa

■ This ad promotes the impact tech companies can have in Africa and here in Nigeria. Many companies have invested in education. However, one may wonder about the limits of such an investment: should education be financed by such companies? Is this philanthropic action truly selfless?

Source : bit.ly/video_DNA

■ Africa is a young continent in terms of learning innovation. That's the reason why it is going to be a unique challenge for companies to operate in a market space which is currently relatively uncontested. There is a need for the African youth to be empowered, and many companies have understood that.

→ Learn more about "Digital – Nation Africa" programme: bit.ly/PbacAMC1re_1b

3 Knowledge, a key asset for self-made men?

En bref *Knowledge creation has always taken a special part in English-speaking countries. The myth of the self-made man or woman creating his or her own business through knowledge is still embedded in the American mindset. To what extent is knowledge also the fruit of experience or individual initiative?*

I Self-made man or woman

1 Part of the American Dream

- Often linked with the notion of the "American Dream", the myth of the "self-made man" was coined by Henry Clay in 1842 to describe someone from an underprivileged background who has economically and socially succeeded through personal experience and innovation rather than outside conditions (inherited fortune, for example).
- This concept has been criticised because the environment that surrounds the self-made man or woman (family, education…) has concrete consequences on his or her career. Being hard-working and climbing the social ladder is an American value.
- There are many rags-to-riches stories of self-made men or women who became entrepreneurs. Starting a small business that thrives and becomes an empire is the case of Steve Jobs who is the co-founder of Apple and the inventor of iPhones.

2 Creation, sharing and innovation

- Professionals are also creators of knowledge. Podcasts, MOOCs are new ways to share new knowledge. For example, NPR (National Public Radio in the USA) has a wide range of political and economics podcasts that 65% of Americans listen to.

> **INFO**
> A **MOOC** (massive open online course) is an online course with an unlimited access and open to everyone, promoting interactive courses.

- Solo podcasts are a new way to produce knowledge for individual users. It is also the case for video makers, bloggers, vloggers, YouTubers, digital influencers. Thinking differently is one of the major goals of these new news providers, giving other perspectives and thus decolonising learning, making it global.

II Knowledge exchange and sharing

1 Exchange of knowledge

- Knowledge creation is the interaction between knowledge and knowing. The more people interact, the more they create new knowledge. That's the reason why there are a lot of partnerships between universities and firms. It can create new knowledge in endless combinations. Empirical method is used to achieve this goal.

- World's unprecedented new changes (organisational, demographic, climatic) lead people to learn new skills from basic education to adult learning: it is **upskilling and reskilling**.
- Partnerships between higher education institutions (HEIs) and firms mediated by students' curricular internships allow increased mutual benefits in the form of the exchange of knowledge and innovation.

KEYWORDS

Upskilling and reskilling mean to improve the skills or to teach new skills to workers or to the unemployed, usually through training.

2 Silicon Valley, a place of creation

- The headquarters of Apple, Apple Park, are located in Silicon Valley (South of San Francisco). It is the home of many high-tech corporations. Silicon Valley is a privileged place for high technology and innovation. → MÉMO VISUEL
- Stanford University (also located in Silicon Valley, Santa Clara County) has played a major role in the growth of the area, where significant computer science departments were developed at multiple universities.

zoOm

TED, a new aid

Source : bit.ly/video_TED

- The very first TED Talks were conferences and later videos from experts on Technology, Entertainment and Design. TED was created by Richard Saul Wurman in 1984.
- Now, they are inspirational talks and influential videos that tackle the subjects about transmitting knowledge, education, politics, sciences... under the slogan "ideas worth spreading". More than 3,800 TED Talks have been posted worldwide in 2020-2021 with subtitles in more than 100 languages.

→ Discover all TED Talks: bit.ly/PbacAMC1re_1c

4 Digital education

En bref *Digitalisation is providing new opportunities and new techniques in the classrooms as it provides answers to some geographical, social and financial problems. The recent pandemic has accelerated this trend: e-learning and online tools are more than ever under the spotlight. What are the challenges raised by e-learning?*

I Revolution of universal knowledge

1 The rise of online learning

- Schools and education in English-speaking countries have changed a lot with the arrival of new technologies, providing an enormous amount of information just a click away and widening the scope of learning opportunities and adapting to different learning styles.

- **The Open University** in the UK, the Khan Academy in the US, MOOCs, podcasts, e-books, online classes and degrees are a few ways technology has invaded education and become an asset to gain new skills.

> **INFO**
> **The Open University** was created in 1969 in the UK. It is a pioneer of distance learning, offering free classes across 200 qualifications.

- The use of technology has changed the way we see the classroom. The teacher that used to be the main source of knowledge, now shares the stage with online resources. The Covid-19 pandemic has accelerated the rise of e-learning that was used globally to counter the spread of the virus. Teachers had no choice but to revert to innovative distance learning techniques to assess the students and lead interactive activities.

2 Reshaping education

- Technology has changed the way students learn and share that learning. Thanks to these new tools, students can collaborate on projects using Google Docs. Technology has developed new forms of communication and collaboration. AI is already used in order to help develop skills and testing systems by providing personalised learning, granting universal access to knowledge or identifying classroom weaknesses.

- Online and distance learning also provide an answer to obstacles in parts of the world where access to school is not easy. In rural India for instance, online education has been a remedy to the lack of infrastructures.

- In South Africa, the government piloted e-learning experiments in some schools located in townships, issuing tablets to students and smart boards to teachers in order to facilitate the learning process. As a result, student performances have improved.

II Limits to e-learning

1 Screen time and sociability

■ Despite a greater flexibility and autonomy in their learning process, students encounter many challenges with online classes: difficulty to focus, lagging in their work, lack of motivation and social interaction. When the material becomes more difficult, it gets harder for students to rely on their self-study to understand the course.

■ Another major issue is screen time and the health issue for younger learners. It is a well-known fact that too much screen time can have serious effects on their sight, weight, but also sleep and mental health.

2 Digital inequalities

■ A digital education requires having access to new technologies, to electricity and some expensive material. Yet, access to all this is not possible for everyone.

■ Digital illiteracy and "homework gap" are two key obstacles in e-learning as children – and their families – don't have enough knowledge to use computers. This results in difficulties at home for students with technology deficient backgrounds.

zoOm

The Khan Academy

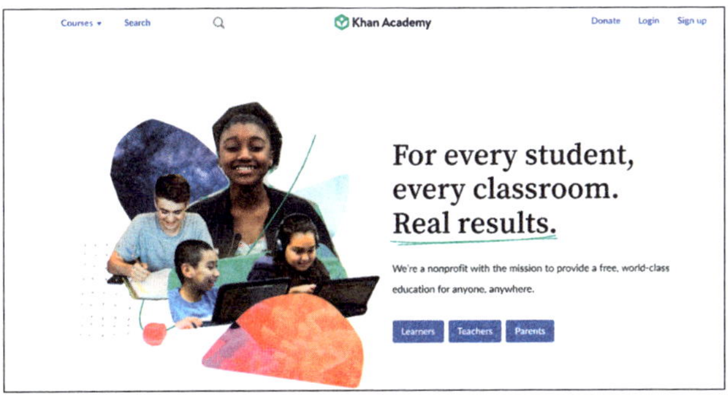

■ Sal Khan founded the Khan Academy in 2007. While he worked as a hedge fund analyst, he started tutoring his cousins via Yahoo and YouTube, which gave him the idea to open the online academy.

■ The Khan Academy, an American non-profit educational institution, offers free online classes in a variety of subjects. It has exponentially grown since 2007. It focuses on its ability to provide a personalised programme for each student, guaranteeing results.

→ Learn more about the Khan Academy: bit.ly/PbacAMC1re_1d

MÉMO VISUEL

Learning in English-speaking countries

Different and unequal schooling systems

- **Public / private** sectors
- **Uniform** (except for the USA)
- Personal **achievement** rewarded in US schools
- Educational **divides**

How to gain and share knowledge?

- Learning more and differently: **upward mobility**
- Podcasts, vloggers & digital influencers
- **Brain gain** and **brain drain**

PRODUCING SHARING

Supporting

University partnership

- Universities: learning and **research**
- **Brain circulation**: mobility of highly skilled researchers
- Cambridge Africa Programme

Business plan for R & D

- **Investing** in education = brand loyalty, developing new tools
- Merchandising education
- **R & D**, a key for economic, environmental and social development

AND KNOWLEDGE

Taking advantage of knowledge

Knowledge, a story of a lifetime

- **The American Dream**: working, gaining knowledge and experience to succeed
- **Rags-to-riches stories** about self-made men and entrepreneurs

Sharing knowledge and experience

- **Partnerships** universities / firms
- **Upskilling** and **reskilling**
- **Silicon Valley** and **Stanford University**: places of avant-garde creators

Inventing new ways of teaching

Revolution of universal knowledge

- **Adaptability** to different learning profiles
- **Collaborative documents**, AI, remote learning

Limits to e-learning

- Lack of motivation and social interaction
- **Health issues**
- **Digital literacy**: skills required to learn and work in a society that revolves around technology

SE TESTER QUIZ

Vérifiez que vous avez bien compris les points clés des **fiches 1 à 4**.

1 Educational systems in English-speaking countries

→ FICHE 1

1. Reliez les débuts de phrase à leur fin.

a. An English public school •   • is state-funded.
b. An American public school •   • is not state-funded.
c. An American private school •   • is not state-funded.

2. Cochez la réponse qui convient.

What is the main disadvantage of distant learning or leaning with robots?

☐ a. They create brain drain.
☐ b. They create upward mobility.
☐ c. They create social and/or racial divides.

2 Research, experimentation and development

→ FICHE 2

Vrai ou faux ? Cochez la case qui convient.

	V	F
a. Brain circulation aims at transferring students abroad easily.	☐	☐
b. Cambridge is a hub for scientific research.	☐	☐
c. Tech companies have invested heavily in education.	☐	☐

3 Knowledge, a key asset for self-made men?

→ FICHE 3

Complétez le texte ci-dessous avec les mots qui conviennent.

A self-made man or woman is someone who has economically .... through .... experience and hard .... and who is usually from an .... social background. This concept is often linked to the .... Dream. To succeed, he or she has to think .... and offer something new.

4 Digital education

→ FICHE 4

Cochez la ou les réponse·s qui convien·nen·t.

1. In what ways can developing countries benefit from online education?

☐ a. It compensates for a lack of infrastructure.
☐ b. It helps children's performance.

2. What is the paradox of digital education?

☐ a. It helps students acquire new skills, but it can lead to a lack of motivation.
☐ b. It helps students acquire autonomy, but it doesn't ruin social interaction.
☐ c. It doesn't help students sleep better, but it allows them to have better grades.

S'ENTRAÎNER

5 Réviser le cours en 8 questions flash

→ FICHES 1 à 4

1. What are two types of inequalities that school systems face?
2. What is the difference between brain drain and brain gain?
3. What are the advantages of studying in a research institution?
4. Why would businesses invest in education?
5. What is a rags-to-riches story?
6. What is the difference between upskilling and reskilling?
7. How has technology reshaped education?
8. What does "digital illiteracy" mean?

6 Analyser un graphique

→ FICHE 4

Observez le graphique, puis répondez aux questions.

Document A

This bar chart, published by the Pew Research Center, shows that in the USA, many adults are not deeply familiar with some major digital learning concepts and platforms.

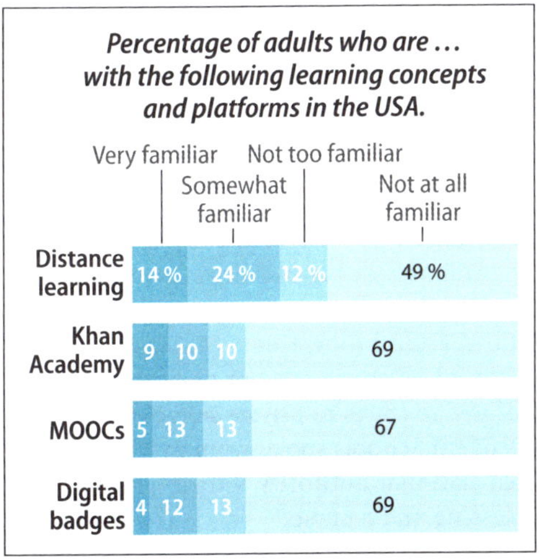

INFO
"Digital badges" or **"e-badges"** are indicators of an accomplishment, a skill, a quality that you have gained through learning and given by a learning online platform.

1. In two sentences, what does the bar chart show? What do the abscissa (x or horizontal scale) and ordinate (y or vertical scale) of the chart show?
2. Whose point of view is given? Say when and why it is interesting.

7 Comprendre un article de presse

→ FICHES 1 et 4

Lisez le texte et répondez aux questions.

Document B Virtual Learning Means Unequal Learning

This article was published on The Pew Charitable Trusts website. It is a US non-governmental organisation founded in 1948. Its aim is to "serve public interest".

Karen Reyes, who teaches deaf and hard-of-hearing children in Austin, Texas, worries about her first-grade pupils who will be learning online this fall. She's concerned that virtual learning is harder for younger, special needs children, especially those who may not have as much support at home as students in more affluent communities.

"It has brought out a lot of the inequities in our district, especially in special education," Reyes said of the distance learning program.

In her school, 93% of the students are considered economically disadvantaged, according to a city estimate.

"Either one or both of the parents have to work," said Reyes, 31, who also is a leader in the local American Federation of Teachers chapter, in a phone interview. "That makes it even harder because small children need adults with them when they are learning."

By contrast, in affluent Howard County, Maryland, in the outer Washington, D.C., suburbs, which is also going to virtual classes in the fall, many parents are scrambling to line up tutors to help their kids. Families also are banding together to form "pods" of children, with tutors whose rates can range from $70 an hour for tutoring one child to $29 an hour each for a pod of four. [...]

School districts that can afford it are trying to help. Some are giving or loaning laptops to students who don't have them. Others are giving out Wi-Fi hotspots so that children can get online. [...]

The inequity is even more stark between public and private schools. Many smaller private schools with large campuses or big buildings have the ability and resources to spread students out in classrooms. Many regions report a run on private school applications. South Carolina Gov. Henry McMaster, a Republican, sparked an uproar and a lawsuit when he tried to dedicate a portion of the federal stimulus money allocated to states to private school vouchers.

National Association of Independent Schools spokeswoman Myra McGovern said the lack of a centralized national authority setting policy for all schools, public and private, is a blessing and a curse.

"Having a national standard or guidelines could make things a lot less confusing," she said in a phone interview.

Elaine S. Povich, www.pewtrusts.org, July 29th, 2020,
Stateline, an initiative of The Pew Charitable Trusts.

1. Give another expression for "virtual learning". Explain what virtual learning creates amongst children and say why.

2. Say who is impacted, and spot the consequences of distant learning on children.

3. Identify the solutions and drawbacks that the article offers, and list them in the table below. Then write a short text to present the solutions and insist on the paradox.

CONSEIL
Pensez à mentionner le ton de l'article ou si l'auteur·e marque un parti pris, même léger, et c'est le cas ici.

Solutions	Drawbacks
•	• ....
•	• ....
•	• ....

8 Traduction en français

Répondez aux questions préparatoires puis traduisez l'article publié sur le site de Pew Charitable Trusts de « Karen Reyes, who teaches... » à « distance learning program. » (document B, l. 1-7).

1. En vous aidant du contexte, choisissez la meilleure traduction pour traduire « first-grade pupils » (l. 2).

☐ a. élèves en première année

☐ b. élèves en primaire

☐ c. élèves en CP

2. Même question pour « special needs children » (l. 3-4).

☐ a. enfants dans le besoin

☐ b. enfants aux besoins spécifiques

☐ c. enfants handicapés

3. Même question pour « more affluent communities » (l. 5).

☐ a. d'un environnement / d'un milieu plus favorisé

☐ b. d'une communauté plus affluente

☐ c. d'une communauté plus influente

CONSEIL
Pour la première phrase, évitez de traduire mot à mot « qui enseigne à des enfants ». Proposez une transposition. → FICHE 32

OBJECTIF BAC

9 Synthèse de documents • Online education challenges

3 h

Les deux documents A (p. 19) et B (p. 20) que vous venez d'étudier et le document qui va suivre (C) constituent le dossier à analyser pour l'épreuve de synthèse portant sur la thématique « Savoirs, création, innovation » et plus particulièrement l'axe « Production et circulation des savoirs ».

LE SUJET

Prenez connaissance du dossier proposé, composé des documents A, B et C non hiérarchisés, et traitez en anglais le sujet suivant (500 mots maximum) :

Taking into account their specificities, show how the documents illustrate the challenges of online education in the English-speaking world.

Document C What new problems digitised classrooms create

This article offers an example about how online teaching is widening the gender gap and creating serious challenges in India.

Online education has become common during the pandemic. For young Indian women, this trend goes along with serious new challenges. [...]

Online teaching and learning presented some important advantages. The costs and efforts spent on commuting were reduced. Classes were often recorded, so students had access to a lesson even if they missed it. [...] Notwithstanding these advantages, online teaching presented enormous challenges. In particular, it deepened the existing inequalities in society regarding class and gender. [...] In India, for instance, one third of the families live in one-room houses. [...] Moreover, a family with more than one student would need more devices, and access to the devices depends on gender in various ways:

• First, in patriarchal and gender unequal societies like India, the boys will almost always have preferential access.

• Second, in 2018, not even 13 % of women in India were able to operate a computer compared with about 20 % of men. In the rural areas, the percentage of women able to use computers was close to half of that of men. Their ability to grasp opportunities is obviously impaired. [...]

Domestic violence

There is yet another dimension to the gendered nature of online education. UN agencies report increased domestic violence, calling it a "shadow pandemic". This is particularly evident in societies with high levels of violence against women. […] Moreover, fear of sexual harassment in public spaces discourages many women from going to cybercafes. In such contexts, academic pursuits are discarded[1]. […]

Educational institutions must recognise that several 'worlds' co-exist around the virtual classroom screen. As online education is delivered now, the assumption is that real and virtual classrooms are basically the same. This assumption is wrong. A physical classroom, despite its diversities and complexities, creates a framework of equality. The online classroom is far more steeped in[2] the realities of a discriminatory world, especially for women. […]

Educators need to acknowledge this and improve matters. The responses will have to be context-specific. They could include institution-led, gender-responsive initiatives. […] The state has an enormous role in recognising the gender disparities in online education. Governments must launch initiatives such as prioritised provision of devices and internet access to women and girls. Civil-society organisations have been proactive in their commitment to a gender-equal world. It is time now to take it to another level that encourages women's education in this changed scenario.

Ipsita Sapra, www.dandc.eu,
September 22th 2021.

1. discarded: rejected
2. steeped in: rooted in

▶▶▶ LA FEUILLE DE ROUTE

→ Reportez-vous à la méthode générale de la synthèse de documents, p. 128-129.

Étape 1 Analyser les termes du sujet

- *Challenges :* ce terme est polysémique, il peut avoir une connotation positive ou négative. À vérifier en analysant les documents.
- *Online education :* pensez à séparer les deux termes. Dans un premier temps, *education* : on parle alors de l'école, la façon d'apprendre, le succès. Dans un deuxième temps, on s'intéresse spécifiquement à ce qui est *online*, donc à l'utilisation des nouvelles technologies.

Étape 2 Lire et analyser le corpus à la lumière de la problématique

- List the different divides mentioned or suggested in the three documents.
- List the negative and positive aspects of digital education in the corpus.

Problématique : What are the social and cultural consequences of digital education?

Étape 3 Analyser et comparer l'apport de chaque document

	Class / social divide	Gender divide / special needs	Generation gap
Doc. A Chart			digital literacy of adults
Doc. B Online article	• rush to private schools in the US • wealthy parents can provide their children with computer / tuitions	deaf and children in young age need adults to learn	
Doc. C Online article	• one-room apartment • more than 2 children in the household = need more computers	• access to computers • domestic violence • sexual harassment → girls don't go to cybercafés	parents can't help because of digital illiteracy in India

Étape 4 Construire le plan de la synthèse

I. Widening the social and generational gaps

II. Minorities hit hard

III. A new light on online education

Étape 5 Rédiger la synthèse → CORRIGÉ p. 27

CORRIGÉS

SE TESTER QUIZ

1 Educational systems in English-speaking countries

1. a. An English public school is not state-funded.
b. An American public school is state-funded.
c. An American private school is not state-funded.
2. Réponse c. Distant learning or learning with robots create social and/or racial divides, as the less privileged you are, the harder it is to buy a computer or any other devices. It is also more difficult for impaired children.

2 Research, experimentation and development

a. Faux. Brain circulation aims at the mobility of researchers in order to create an international network.
b. Faux. Cambridge is a hub for interdisciplinary research, nor just science.
c. Vrai. Tech companies have pledged millions of dollars, equipping schools, developing new tools...

INFO
Big **tech companies** invest millions of dollars in education. They focus on STEM, but also coding and computer science education. In summer 2021, they have also pledge $100 million to fight racial injustice through education.

3 Knowledge, a key asset for self-made men?

A self-made man or woman is someone who has economically succeeded through personal experience and hard work and who is usually from an underprivileged social background. This concept is often linked to the American Dream. To succeed, he or she has to think differently and offer something new.

4 Digital education

1. Réponses a et b. In India, for example, online teaching is a substitute for the lack of schools. It also helps provide a more personalised learning and help children's performance.
2. Réponse a. Despite acquiring new skills, digital education has drawbacks such as a lack of motivation, social interaction and sleep.

S'ENTRAÎNER

5 Réviser le cours en 8 questions flash

1. Schools are often confronted with social, gender, racial, economic or even geographical inequalities.
2. When a country receives a highly-qualified immigrant, it is called brain gain, while it is called brain drain for the sending country.
3. Studying in a research institution allows students to have access to up-to-date data and efficient teaching. In addition, both students and teachers get to use state-of-the-art facilities and receive funding.
4. Businesses, and in particular big tech companies, would invest in education because they are hoping to create brand loyalty. Moreover, it generates good revenue, image, and it participates in the development of a nation's technological skills.
5. A rags-to-riches story is the story of a man or woman from a poor background who has become rich through his/her work and experience.
6. Upskilling means to improve what a worker knows, the skills s/he already has. Reskilling means that a worker is taught new skills so that s/he will be better at his/her jobs and might have a better salary.

7. Technology has made it easier to create collaborative work and have a more personalised learning process thanks to AI. However, the use of technology has modified the place of the teacher in a classroom.
8. Digital illiteracy is the lack of skills to use a computer, creating inequalities between those who have access and know how to use a computer and those who don't.

6 Analyser un graphique

1. The graph shows how familiar American adults are with new forms of learning / online learning concepts or platforms. The x-axis shows the degree of knowledge the adults have on them, and the y-axis shows four different new ways of learning. Adults are **not too or at all familiar** with new forms of learning.
2. The point of view of adults is given, therefore it is also the point of view of parents struggling with new forms of learning. The graph dates back before the pandemic (2016), which shows that American adults were not really prepared for such a situation.

INFO
The Covid-19 pandemic has (un)fortunately revealed the lack of e-training of adults.

7 Comprendre un article de presse

1. Distant learning (= another expression) creates inequality amongst pupils / children. Underprivileged families can't afford to buy computers or are less likely to offer them help.
2. Deaf, hard-of-hearing, poor children are impacted by the use of distant learning. Private schools can face pandemic with bigger facilities and better resources. Finally, children with rich parents can afford private tuitions.
3. *Voici le tableau complété.*

Solutions	Drawbacks
• a national curriculum • lending laptops • wi-fi hotspots	• gaps in funding • apprehension • inequity

A national standard (= curriculum) would be a solution. Schools can lend laptops to students who don't have any. Others are giving out wi-fi hotspots so that children can get online. Rep. Gov. gives federal money to private sector, thus creating a new gap. Finally, distant learning supposedly aims at helping children during the pandemic, yet it is a source of apprehension and iniquity amongst parents and children. The tone of the article reinforces this idea. The journalist is biased and takes side with what Karen Reyes thinks about distant learning.

8 Traduction en français

1. Réponse c. « En primaire » est trop vague et « en première année » sous-entend à l'université.
2. Réponse b. « Handicapés » est un faux sens et « dans le besoin » peut être perçu comme un contresens.

3. Réponse a. Utiliser le mot « communauté » est un calque, voire un faux sens, et « affluent » est un faux ami.

Voici la traduction proposée.

Karen Reyes, enseignante auprès d'enfants sourds et malentendants à Austin, au Texas, s'inquiète pour ses élèves de cours préparatoire qui vont devoir suivre des cours à distance cet automne. Elle est préoccupée, car l'apprentissage à distance est plus ardu pour les plus petits et pour ceux qui ont des besoins éducatifs spécifiques, plus particulièrement ceux qui ne reçoivent pas autant d'aide chez eux / à la maison que des élèves issus d'un milieu / d'un environnement plus favorisé.

> **CONSEIL**
> Faites la différence entre *iniquities* et *inequalities*. Le terme « iniquités » aurait été possible mais, peu utilisé en français, on lui préfère « inégalités sociales ».

« Cela met en évidence beaucoup d'inégalités sociales à l'échelle de notre quartier, en particulier dans l'enseignement spécialisé, » déclare Karen Reyes à propos du plan mis en place pour l'enseignement à distance.

OBJECTIF BAC

9 Synthèse de documents • Online education challenges

Les titres en couleur et les puces permettent de mettre en évidence la structure du corrigé mais ils ne figureraient pas sur une copie de bac.

Introduction

Online education has been trendy for the past ten years, shuffling the way we think about education, teachers and the learning process. Despite some unequivocal positive aspects, online teaching has also raised many concerns. What are the social and cultural consequences of online education? The three documents shed a rather negative light on online education but offer some kind of positive outcome as well.

Widening the social and generational gaps

- The documents stress how online education has shed **a new light on inequalities** and has raised new questions about equal opportunities for all children.
- The extent of **digital illiteracy** became obvious with the pandemic. The graph (A) and the article (C) tackle this issue for adults in the US and for girls in India who are less likely to know how to use a computer or know about online tools, platforms and resources.
- Similarly, the two articles (B and C) highlight **the widening social and class gap**. Both articles point at the inequities that exist and that have become more apparent with online education. Document B opposes wealthy parents who can afford to pay for tutors and computers to families who can't. Document C focuses on lower-class Indian families who live in crowded one-bedroom apartments where children don't have space to work.

Minorities hit hard

■ The article about India (C) insists on the gender inequalities that have surged with the pandemic and the switch to online teaching. In addition to poor living conditions, girls face other challenges with online education.

■ Two major themes are mentioned in article C: domestic violence and sexual harassment. Indeed, girls face domestic expectations and must take care of the chores in the house before getting to the online classes. At least, schools provided a safer environment for them to learn.

■ The article about the United States also points at a minority that has suffered from virtual classes: the deaf and hearing-impaired. Indeed, **special needs students** are usually offered help at school that they are not getting during virtual classes.

> **INFO**
> **Special needs students** can have a variety of disabilities or learning difficulties. Many programs exist in schools to help them and give them equal opportunities to succeed.

A new light on online teaching

■ Despite the appalling consequences for girls in India or deaf children in poor areas, virtual classes have revealed inequalities that were hidden or at least less obvious before.

■ Document B showcases the solidarity that can be found in some communities: some school districts are bridging the gap by loaning computers or laptops, giving access to wi-fi hotspots, etc.

■ In India (C), the government and associations are trying to find solutions. They are aware of the situation and despite a strong class and gender divide, they are trying to launch initiatives to counter gender inequalities.

Conclusion

If, at first sight, the documents seem to be offering a dark vision of online education and its new challenges, it is also clear that the articles are raising awareness on deeply-rooted issues that surfaced with the pandemic and the switch to online teaching. It is time for governments, associations and parents to face them and find sustainable solutions.

(485 words)

2 Science and techniques, promises and challenges

NFTs are unique digital files which revolutionise the art world. This digital collage by Beeple was sold 69 million dollars at Christie's.

5 From inventions to innovations

En bref *Science has always been a key factor for changes. Inventing is a never-ending process bringing innovations at the core of our lives. Innovating is a challenge involving or opposing men, ideas and countries. To what extent has the English-speaking world been the cradle of our ever-changing society?*

I From an idea to a concept

1 Inventing

- Inventing means imagining, creating something new. Patenting an invention documents, through a legal process, the fact that the inventor was the first one to have the idea.

- Cerebration (shared thinking and collaboration) seems to be a key component of research and scientific breakthroughs. This is what makes iconic institutions like the MIT (Massachusetts Institute of Technology) or places like the Silicon Valley in California great hubs for innovations.

- Some ideas are developed over several decades or even centuries. For example, the use of compressed air as means of propelling vehicles was discovered as early as 1799, but came into being only two centuries later with the **Hyperloop** project.

> **INFO**
> The **Hyperloop** uses pods to transport passengers through low-pressure tubes at a top speed of 750mph using magnetic levitation to reduce friction.

2 Innovating

- Scientific improvements, along with an evolution of mentalities, are a constant source of inspiration which transforms some inventions into innovations. Answering a need, an innovation is an evolutionary change to an existing process or product, often synonym with commercial usefulness.

- Companies such as Google, Microsoft, Apple, Tesla and Facebook (now Meta) innovate for business and thanks to business. Thus Apple's former CEO Steve Jobs can be considered as a poster child for innovation (= the personification of).

II The race to the top

1 Pioneering Britain

- Britain was the cradle of the industrial revolution in the 18th century. The British Empire soon emerged as a leading power and became the "workshop of the world". Scottish engineer James Watt's steam engine (1765) revolutionised transport and industry.

■ From the 16th to the 18th century the emergence of the cloth industry in England favoured the birth of capitalism where accumulated capital was invested to increase productivity and profit. Liberalism, based on individual rights, civil liberties and democracy, emphasised the importance of free market and freedom of entrepreneurship.

■ The USA soon joined the UK at the forefront of a new dynamics. American inventor Thomas Edison earned more than 1,000 patents including the phonograph, the motion picture camera and the light bulb (1879).

2 A worldwide competition

■ Countries have always wanted to shine and reach the best economic competitiveness. This need for recognition has triggered many innovations, blooming at the CES.

> **INFO**
> The CES (**Consumer Electronics Show** in Las Vegas, USA) hosts the world's most influential technology event, where business and innovations are as one.

■ The space race between the USA and the Soviet Union is one of the best examples. This race to technological superiority turned into unprecedented scientific and engineering collaboration of 15 countries when the construction of the ISS (International Space Station) started in 1998.

■ Since the 1960s robots have revolutionised industry. Artificial Intelligence is now at the core of the competition, transforming people's lives and industries by implementing data exchange, cloud computing and cyber-physical systems in industry 4.0. The USA emerged once again as the front-runner of the AI industry, with China ranking second.

zoOm

The Unimate

■ American inventor and entrepreneur George Devol spent his life transforming real ideas into products. He teamed up with American engineer Joseph Engelberger to start the first robot manufacturing company, Unimation.

■ Patented in 1961, the Unimate was the first programmable industrial robot installed on a General Motors car assembly line. That hydraulic manipulator arm could perform repetitive tasks. This paved the way to the third industrial revolution which implemented automation, computers and electronics as core elements of the industry.

→ Learn more about the history of robotics : bit.ly/PbacAMC1re_2a

6 Threatening scientific innovations

En bref *Science has come to the rescue ever since men needed support. From glasses to pacemakers, technology has made life easier and safer. But new trends like transhumanism and augmented men may turn science into a dangerous asset. We can wonder if limits to innovations should be set.*

I When science makes the world change

1 Discovering

From Edward Jenner's first vaccine in 1798 to Dolly, the first mammal to be cloned from an adult cell by a Scottish scientist in 1996, scientific breakthroughs opened up a lot of possibilities in biology and medicine. Thus men live longer.

2 Pushing the limits

- Men are now replaced by robots or drones in hazardous jobs or perilous rescues. Exoskeletons revolutionise the industry and the army, enabling heavy loads to be carried.
- Robots have become high-skilled surgeons. Scientists create cutting-edge prosthetics for amputees or physically-impaired people that can walk again. Bionic limbs can now be controlled by the patient's thoughts.
- South African-born American entrepreneur and engineer Elon Musk's Neuralink project aims at merging humans with Artificial Intelligence to cure the after-effects of some diseases.

INFO
Monkey Pong is **Neuralink's** latest experiment. It shows a monkey with a brain-machine interface (BMI) playing the video game Pong with its mind.

II Science is a double-edged tool

1 Going too far?

- Genetically modified organisms are animals or plants whose structure has been changed by scientists to be produced more effectively. But danger is looming when these GMOs multiply, changing the very nature of biodiversity.
- Autonomous cars are at the core of car innovations. This may go fast or too far as in case of an accident it is hard to say if the engineer, the car maker or the driver should be held responsible. Even legislation has no answer. Are we beyond limits of reasoning ?

2 Supervising science?

■ Innovations and economic growth lead the way towards a future where science seems limitless. But can scientists invent anything? Should research be more regulated and supervised? **Ethics** is now part of all science curriculum because scientists have a moral and ethical responsibility in carrying out an experiment or not.

> **KEY WORD**
> **Ethics** is based on moral principles that govern a person's behaviour or how they conduct an activity.

■ Over the past decades the USA and England have been at the forefront of innovations in medicine and sciences, always keeping an eye on ethics. They have developed new law to answer the challenges presented by these scientific break-throughs. The International Bioethics Committee (IBC), created in 1993, is a global forum for reflection in bioethics. It aims at ensuring respect for human dignity and freedom.

■ Cloning refers to techniques of copying genetic information. The cloning of the sheep Dolly opened up a lot of possibilities. But even if human cloning has been possible since the 2010s, it is unethical and remains illegal. Transhumanism appeals to more and more people who dream of eternal digital life. Would that be ethical?

zoOm

Isaac Asimov and the laws of robotics

■ When American science fiction author Isaac Asimov popularised the term "robotics", he gave birth to robot ethics. In 1942 he introduced the three laws of robotics in his short story *Runaround*. These laws, meant to define how robots should interact with humans, have been the anchor points of scientific research.

■ In 1950, some of Asimov's short stories were published as a book in *I, Robot*. Inspired by Asimov, the film *I, Robot* was released in 2004, starring Will Smith. This 2035 dystopian world chronicles intelligent humanoid robots working along with humans, following Asimov's laws.

→ Watch the trailer of *I, Robot* : bit.ly/PbacAMC1re_2b

7 A better place to live

En bref *From transportation to an overwhelming digital world, the evolution of society has impacted the planet, for better or for worse. Climate change is the biggest issue. To what extent can science lead the way and be an asset in preserving a planet science has jeopardised?*

I Facing two major issues

1 Favouring green transportation

- In 2019, 29% of greenhouse gas emissions came from transportation in the USA, resulting from burning of fossil fuels. The need for change has made transportation go greener. From electric cars to green buses, cities are trying to prolong the unprecedented positive impact Covid-19 has had on greenhouse gas emissions. In 2020, New York has emerged as the leading US city for green transportation with the most sustainable transportation system.
- American company Uber focuses on air flying taxis and drone deliveries to make cities breathe. In 2021 President Biden announced half of new vehicles sold in the US should be electric by 2030.

2 Developing sustainable energies

- Sustainable energies are eco-friendly and available widely free of cost. They are the key to a renewable future where fossil fuels shouldn't be used any more to decrease the emission of carbon dioxide. The use of solar, wind, hydropower, geothermal and ocean energies meet today's demand of energy and don't cause any harm to the environment.
- Scotland has implemented massive floating offshore wind farms to boost its production of energy. Europe is targeting a 55% reduction of CO_2 emissions by 2030, aiming at climate neutrality by 2050.

KEY FIGURE
Solar energy is projected to skyrocket from 11% of total US renewable energy to 48% by 2050.

- President Joe Biden has taken the USA back into the game after former President Trump had left the 2015 COP 21 Paris agreement. In June 2021 Biden challenged American workers and industry to tackle the climate crisis, aiming at reaching net zero emissions economy-wide by 2050.

II Improving city life

1 From smart houses to smart cities

- For the past few years connectivity has been a key feature to make impactful energy choices. Smart houses are wonders of the 21st century designed to save energy with devices such as water-saving skills, smart electric panels or energy-efficient insulation. The **IoT** helps keep track of your lifestyle not to spend energy you don't need.

> **INFO**
> The IoT (**Internet of Things**) is a network of physical objects using sensors and software to exchange data.

- Smart cities tackle the growing urbanisation challenges promoting sustainable development practices with information and communication technology. They change the way people work and live.
- Starting with V2I (vehicule-to-infrastructure) which enables vehicles to communicate with infrastructures, smart cities are now focusing on V2X (vehicles-to-everything), enlarging the communication to any entity that can impact or be impacted by a vehicle.

2 The other side of the coin

- However our digital lives create huge amounts of data which have a terrible environmental impact as the Internet accounts for around 10% of global electricity demand and is responsible for almost 1 billion tonnes of greenhouse gas emissions per year (about 3% of total emissions). These emissions are predicted to double by 2025. In 2021 more than 50% of the global population use the Internet, with a peak of 91% in the USA.
- A worker's yearly carbon footprint reaches 135kg from sending emails, which is the equivalent of driving 200 miles. The Internet has as much impact on climate change as the aviation industry.

zoOm

Fighting e-waste

- Over-consumption of tech-hungry nations leads to a global technology crisis. Some multi-billion-dollar companies don't pick up the cost of recycling the devices they sell. This e-waste is mostly dumped in developing countries which can't afford protecting from toxic pollution affecting health and natural resources. Transportation of this e-waste also impacts the environment.
- 57.4 m of electronic waste were discarded in 2021. Only 17.4% were properly recycled. International e-waste Day is celebrated every October 14 to sensitise citizens.

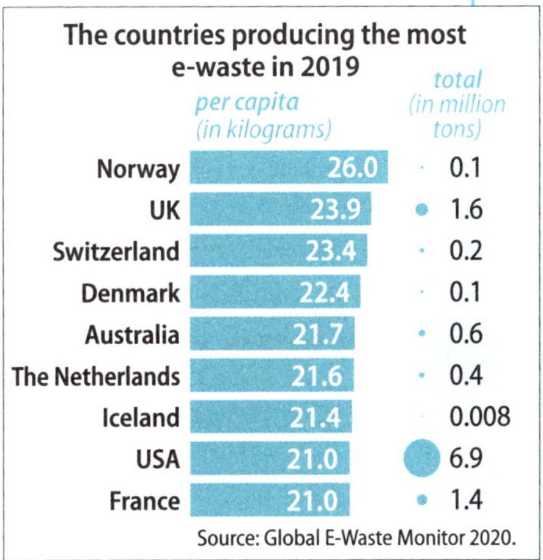

→ Get more information on e-waste Day : bit.ly/PbacAMC1re_2c

8 Art & science

En bref *The closing of venues for live concerts or exhibitions during the pandemic has accelerated the digital trend. Artists find more and more ways of expressing themselves and the public new ways of enjoying art. Museums are boosting the scene of digital art. Can new technologies define a new kind of art?*

I Displaying art

1 Reaching a larger public

■ Today people live stream almost everything. What started as a useful tool for video gamers turned into a worldwide mania. No surprise artists find their public on streaming platforms such as YouTube Live, Facebook, Twitter or Twitch where the community aspect is paramount. Streaming services such as Netflix, Amazon Prime or Apple TV have revolutionised the connection viewers and even film makers have with the cinema.

■ Google Arts and Culture was created in 2011 as the Google Art Project with the objective to make art collections more accessible through digitisation.

> **INFO**
> **Google Arts and Culture** is an online platform offering virtual tours and online collections from 2,500 world-class museums and galleries.

2 New experiences

■ Online art is so accessible we sometimes wonder how museums still attract visitors. They have risen to the challenge, offering more and more immersive and interactive experiences where technology-driven artworks address your senses.

■ Art and entertainment meet in places such as AREA15 in Las Vegas where state-of-the-art technology and immersive activities appeal to the public. From the American Museum of Natural History in New York displaying organisms that glow, blink, flash and glitter in "Creatures of light" to "Immersive Van Gogh" exhibiting 500,000 cubic feet of animated projections, digital art is everywhere using VR (virtual reality), holography and digital projectors.

II New forms of art

1 Art and screens

■ Art, science and technology are at the core of digital art, offering amazing experiences which are popping up all over the world.

■ Digital literature, an emerging genre for decades, deals with writing which is not meant to be printed. Twitterature consists in a series of tweets which make up a novel, with or without interaction with the readers. Hypertext fiction lets the reader choose their own story. Both are created and read on a screen.

- An NFT (Non-Fungible Token) is a digital asset that represents an artwork, music, a video or even an article. You can't touch it but you can own it. NFTs are sold and bought online with **cryptocurrencies**. They are becoming more and more popular because they are one of a kind, with a unique identifying code. Some people spend a lot of money for just owning one of these files.

KEY WORD

A **cryptocurrency** is a digital currency (e.g. bitcoin) impossible to counterfeit. Blockchains store information in chains and ensure the integrity of transactional data.

2 To be or not to be an artwork

- Art innovates when computers take the lead. AI generates different types of artwork. Computoser is an AI algorithm that turns the computer into a music composer. But is this really art when there is no human touch?
- With the Google Art Transfer app, you become a real artist when you apply the characteristics of well-known paintings to your own pictures. But does that make you Francis Bacon?

zoOm

Beeple's NFT

Beeple's collage, *Everydays: The First 5,000 Days*, 2021, seen on a smartphone.

- Mike Winkelman – the digital artist known as Beeple – has 2.5 million followers across social networks. Through his project *Everydays*, he has created and published a new digital work every day for 14 years.
- He has become world famous since he sold this NFT of his work for $69 million at Christie's in March 2021. With this sales he is ranking in the top three most valuable living artists.

→ Get more information about Beeple : bit.ly/PbacAMC1re_2d

MÉMO VISUEL

SCIENCES AND PROMISES AND

How science goes forward

From inventions to innovations

- **Inventing**: imagining something new
- **Innovating**: answering a need, commercially viable
- Innovative hubs: MIT, Silicon Valley, CES

The Silicon Valley: at the core of US innovation

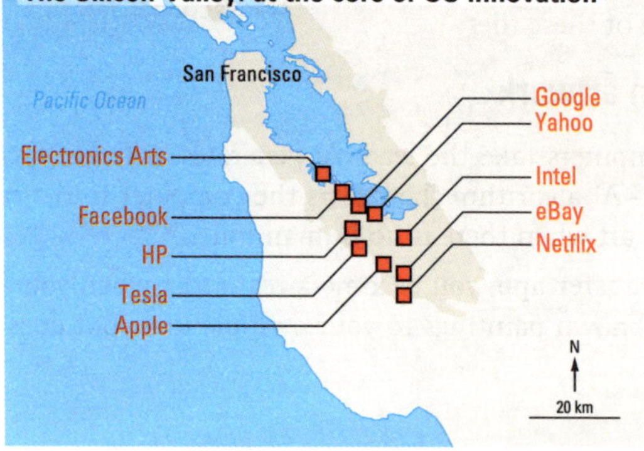

A worldwide competition

- 18th century: **industrial revolution** in Britain
- Capitalism and liberalism
- **Competition** (Space Race) or **collaboration** (ISS)
- **Industry 4.0** (AI)

A double-edged tool?

A helpful science…

- Scientific **breakthroughs**: vaccine (1798), Dolly the clone (1996), etc.
- **Enhancing bodies**: exoskeletons, prosthetics, bionic limbs
- Brain-machine interface

… which goes too far?

- Will we go too far with **GMOs**?
- Who is responsible of a car crash involving an **autonomous car**?
- Should science be more careful with **ethics**?

TECHNIQUES, CHALLENGES

A better place to live

New technologies for a better city

- **Green transportation**
- **V2X**: communication between cars, infrastructures, buildings and people
- Smart houses and smart cities
- **Environmental impact** of data

When science must fix its mistakes

- Growing quantity of **e-waste**
- Emergency to lower **emissions of CO_2**
- Race to saving the planet against **global warming**

Art and science

New ways of displaying art

- Art and entertainment as new form of **museums**
- **Google Arts and Culture**

Picture from the exhibition "Beyond Van Gogh: An Immersive Experience"

New forms of art

- Art, science and technology at the forefront of the **digital art**
- **Interactive** exhibitions and experiences
- **NFT** as the new priceless artwork

SE TESTER QUIZ

Vérifiez que vous avez bien compris les points clés des **fiches 5 à 8**.

1 From inventions to innovations

→ FICHE 5

1. Reliez chaque inventeur à son invention.

a. Thomas Edison •	• steam engine
b. James Watt •	• light bulb
c. Steve Jobs •	• iPhone

2. Vrai ou faux ? Cochez la case qui convient.

	V	F
a. Britain was the world's first most innovative country during the industrial revolution.	☐	☐
b. Unimate, the first industrial robot, was invented in the UK in the 1940s.	☐	☐
c. Industry 4.0 is based on data exchange and cloud computing in smart factories.	☐	☐

2 Threatening scientific innovations

→ FICHE 6

1. Complétez les phrases ci-dessous avec les mots qui conviennent.

a. Isaac Asimov is an American science fiction author who issued the famous three .... of .... in the 1940s.

b. .... consists in copying .... information. It is one of the biggest scientific ...., conveying .... questions.

2. Cochez la ou les propositions qui conviennent.

Bodies can be augmented thanks to...

☐ a. exoskeletons
☐ b. prosthetics
☐ c. Brain-machine interface

3 A better place to live • Art & science

→ FICHES 7 et 8

Trouvez les mots qui correspondent aux définitions suivantes.

a. Electronic devices which are out of order: ....

b. Energy which meets the needs of the present without compromising the needs of future generations: ....

c. Harmful gases, especially carbon dioxide, that prevent heat form the earth escaping into space, causing global warming: ....

d. Digital currency impossible to counterfeit: ....

e. Place where events are hosted: ....

f. Exhibition based on digital projectors: ....

S'ENTRAÎNER

4 Réviser le cours en 8 questions flash

→ FICHES 5 à 8

1. Quote two iconic places for technological innovations in the USA.
2. What is the difference between invention and innovation?
3. Which scientific breakthroughs can change a physically-impaired person's life?
4. Why and how could cloning become dangerous?
5. Which countries are impacted by discarted e-waste and how?
6. What are the main renewable energies?
7. How has Google Arts and Culture changed people's relation to art?
8. Why are NFTs both successful and harmful?

5 Analyser un dessin humoristique

→ FICHE 5

Observez l'image et répondez aux questions.

Document A

"Sir, the robots have gained sentience and are demanding better working conditions."

Robot Bargaining, Drew Panckeri, Weekly Humorist

VOCABULARY
sentience: consciousness

1. Where does the scene take place and who are the two protagonists?
2. The caption means that robots...

☐ a. are not efficient enough in this company.
☐ b. are becoming as intelligent and demanding as humans.
☐ c. have become superior to human workers.

3. What does the cartoonist underline here? Illustrate your answer using what you know about the fear and fascination robots convey.

6 Comprendre un article de presse

→ FICHE 8

Lisez le texte et répondez aux questions.

Document B NFTs may be the future of art — but are they threatening the future of the planet?

NFTs (Non-Fungible Tokens) are unique digital files or assets that are exchanged via cryptocurrency. They can't be touched but some people spend millions to own them.

A digital artist known as Beeple sold a piece of entirely digital art through Christie's for over $69 million in March [2021], flipping the art world upside down. But the digital registry where that piece of art, called an NFT[1], is stored is responsible for the annual emission of more carbon into the atmosphere than most small countries. So why is everyone so eager to jump on the NFT bandwagon? [...]

Artists around the world were thrilled: NFTs provide the opportunity for them to make significant money on their work, reach a broader audience all over the world and link a digital file to a creator, ensuring authenticity. And with the value of cryptocurrency skyrocketing, some think there's never been a better time to get in on it. [...] But recently some artists have started to grapple with the environmental costs of the medium. [...] That's because blockchain technology – which is used by cryptocurrencies like Bitcoin and Ethereum – requires a lot of energy, generating a massive amount of greenhouse gases. In order to "mint"[2] a piece of art on the blockchain and become the official owner, an exorbitant amount of computing power and energy is used to solve complex puzzles in a process known as mining. Ethereum, the open-source blockchain that hosts NFTs, uses a purposely inefficient "proof of work" (PoW) method to create these digital assets. Powerful computers can make an unfathomable[3] number of attempts every second to produce new blocks. Whichever miner gets to the answer first gets their unique asset added to the blockchain. [...] This amount of work is intentional – it creates a competitive market and prevents security threats. But the emissions generated in the process are also contributing to the destruction of Earth'satmosphere. [...]

The financial gains of selling an NFT are tough to ignore, and not just for artists. An NFT of Twitter CEO Jack Dorsey's first-ever tweet sold for $2.9 million. A digital trading card of an epic LeBron James dunk sold for $208,000. [...]

"The environmental issue with NFTs isn't the NFTs themselves, but the way the network they are built on is secured," Shirley [working in a company responsible for several popular blockchain platforms] said. The growing awareness of NFTs'environmental impact comes as evidence piles up about the harmful toll[4] of crypto technology. Annually, Ethereum is currently estimated to consume roughly 44.94 terawatt-hours of electrical energy, which is comparable to the yearly power consumption of countries like Qatar and Hungary. It is responsible for about 21.35 metric tons of carbon dioxide released each year, comparable to the carbon footprint of Sudan. In a recent study, scientists warned Bitcoin alone could push the Earth's temperature 2 degrees Celsius above historical levels, if it were to become as widely adopted as other new technologies. [...]

"What governs the price, part of that is due to media attention," Brendan McGill, co-founder and head of product design and engineering for carbon offset company Offsetra, told CBS News. "Every time Elon Musk tweets about something, the price goes up." Or down.

Sophie Lewis, May 17, 2021, © CBS News.

1. Non-Fungible Token: file that can't be reproduced
2. to mint: to manufacture new coins, new currencies
3. unfathomable: impossible to measure
4. toll: extent of damage

1. What is an NFT? How is it exchanged?

2. What are the reasons why NFTs are a danger for the environment?

3. How can NFTs influence the world's economy? Write your ideas in the table below and use them to write a short paragraph.

Positive sides of NFTs	Negative sides of NFTs
•..	•..
•..	•..
•..	•..
•..	•..
•..	•..

7 Traduction en français

Répondez aux questions préparatoires, puis traduisez l'article de CBS News de « A digital artist » à « the NFT bandwagon? » (document B, l. 1-6).

1. Il faut parfois étoffer la traduction de certains mots pour obtenir une formulation correcte en français. Comment traduiriez-vous « known as » (l. 1) ?

2. L'expression « upside down » vous permet d'inférer le sens de « flip » (l. 2). La phrase étant assez longue, comment pourriez-vous traduire l'expression « flip upside down » par un seul mot ?

CONSEIL
Les deux premières phrases sont très longues. Veillez à opter pour une traduction synthétique de certains mots, expressions ou passages afin de ne pas alourdir votre paragraphe.

OBJECTIF BAC

8 Synthèse de documents • Science and the American nation

3 h

Les deux documents A (p. 41), et B (p. 42-43) que vous venez d'étudier et le document qui va suivre (C) constituent le dossier à analyser pour l'épreuve de synthèse portant sur la thématique « Savoirs, création, innovation » et plus particulièrement l'axe « Sciences et techniques, promesses et défis ».

LE SUJET

Prenez connaissance du dossier proposé, composé des documents A, B et C non hiérarchisés, et traitez en anglais le sujet suivant (500 mots maximum) :

Taking into account their specificities, show how the documents illustrate how science has shaped the American nation and boosted its economy. Make sure to address the positive issues tackled but also the negative sides any scientific breakthrough can introduce.

Document C Extract of President Obama's final State of the Union address – January 12th 2016

Sixty years ago, when the Russians beat us into space, we didn't deny Sputnik was up there. We didn't argue about the science, or shrink our research and development budget. We built a space program almost overnight, and twelve years later, we were walking on the moon.

That spirit of discovery is in our DNA. We're Thomas Edison and the Wright Brothers and George Washington Carver. We're Grace Hopper and Katherine Johnson and Sally Ride. We're every immigrant and entrepreneur from Boston to Austin to Silicon Valley racing to shape a better world. And over the past seven years, we've nurtured that spirit.

We've protected an open Internet, and taken bold new steps to get more students and low-income Americans online. We've launched next-generation manufacturing hubs, and online tools that give an entrepreneur everything he or she needs to start a business in a single day.

But we can do so much more. Last year, Vice President Biden said that with a new moonshot, America can cure cancer. [...] Tonight, I'm announcing a new national effort to get it done. And because he's gone to the mat for all of us, on so many issues over the past forty years, I'm putting Joe in charge of Mission Control. For the loved ones we've all lost, for the family we can still save, let's make America the country that cures cancer once and for all.

Medical research is critical. We need the same level of commitment when it comes to developing clean energy sources. [...]

But even if the planet wasn't at stake; even if 2014 wasn't the warmest year on record – until 2015 turned out even hotter – why would we want to pass up the chance for American businesses to produce and sell the energy of the future?

▶▶▶ LA FEUILLE DE ROUTE

→ *Reportez-vous à la méthode générale de la synthèse de documents, p. 128-129.*

Étape 1 Analyser les termes du sujet

- *How science has shaped the American nation* : influence de la science dans l'effort de construction du pays + spécificité de la nation américaine qui facilite cette évolution.
- *Boosted its economy / positive issues* : atouts scientifiques comme éléments clés de la prospérité et de la supériorité américaines.
- *Negative sides any scientific breakthrough can introduce* : science qui peut nuire, au pays comme à la société en général – question de l'éthique en science.

Étape 2 Lire et analyser le corpus à la lumière de la problématique

- Problématique : To what extent has science shaped the American nation and boosted its economy?
- Analyser chaque document pour en définir le point de vue, en lien avec le développement des États-Unis.
- Relever dans chaque document les points positifs et / ou négatifs liés à cette synergie scientifique.

Étape 3 Analyser et comparer l'apport de chaque document

	Scientific endeavour part of the American Dream	Positive issues boosting the economy	Negative side-effects affecting the USA and the world in general
Doc. A Cartoon	robots = American invention from the 1960s	• robots more and more present in industry • no human failure • high efficiency	• fear of the rise of the robots • robots could take our jobs and overcome humanity • parody
Doc. B Press article		• NFTs revolutionise the art world • blockchain and cryptocurrencies = a competitive market	• digital pollution • cryptocurrencies use a lot of energy • rise of temperature = global warming

Doc. C Speech	• spirit of discovery • famous American inventors and scientists • power of immigration •American Dream of success • national effort	• space race as an asset during the Cold War • more and more access to the Internet • fight against cancer • developing clean energy sources	

Étape 4 Construire le plan de la synthèse

À partir du tableau on peut dégager trois axes pour répondre à la problématique.

I. Science as a backbone of the American Dream.

II. Scientific breakthroughs as assets to shape a dynamic nation over the centuries, boosting its economy.

III. Science as a double-edged tool endangering the nation and the planet.

Étape 5 Rédiger la synthèse → CORRIGÉ p. 49

CORRIGÉS

SE TESTER QUIZ

1 From inventions to innovations

1. a. Thomas Edison : light bulb • b. James Watt : steam engine • c. Steve Jobs : iPhone.

2. a. Vrai. The industrial revolution was born in Britain in the mid-to-late 18th century with the invention of the steam engine and the development of trade.

b. Faux. The Unimate was invented in 1961 by two American scientists: George Devol and Joseph Engelberger.

c. Vrai. Industry 4.0 works thanks to AI, cloud computing and data exchange.

INFO

The invention of the **steam engine** triggered the industrial revolution. From powering huge factories to increasing a transport network, it was synonym with the improvement of technology and productivity.

2 Threatening scientific innovations

1. a. Isaac Asimov is an American science fiction author who issued the famous three laws of robotics in the 1940s.
b. Cloning consists in copying genetic information. It is one of the biggest scientific breakthroughs, conveying ethical questions.
2. Réponses a., b. et c. Augmented bodies are bodies that science makes more efficient, more enduring or better. This can be done thanks to exoskeletons or prosthetics. Brain-machine interfaces enable the brain to communicate with the body.

3 A better place to live

a. Electronic devices which are out of order: e-waste.
b. Energy which meets the needs of the present without compromising the needs of future generations: sustainable energies.
c. Harmful gases, especially carbon dioxide, that prevent heat form the earth escaping into space, causing global warming: greenhouse gas emissions.
d. Digital currency impossible to counterfeit: cryptocurrency.
e. Place where events are hosted: a venue.
f. Exhibition based on digital projectors: an immersive exhibition.

S'ENTRAÎNER

4 Réviser le cours en 8 questions flash

1. The MIT is a private research university near Boston (Massachussetts) focusing on modern technology and science. The Sillicon Valley (San Francisco, California) is home to most of the US tech companies.
2. An invention is something new, which is presented for the first time. An innovation is bettering a concept which already exists, aiming at development and profit.
3. Exoskeletons or BMI can enable physically-impaired people to walk again.
4. Cloning is an important breakthrough as it can help medicine. But human cloning can become dangerous as it could be done to modify human beings. People would always want to be better.
5. Developing countries receive more and more e-waste because some countries don't bother recycling their electronic devices at home. This is a great source of toxicity for the poor workforce demantling it and the natural ressources.

INFO

E-waste contains toxic components such as mercury, lead and lithium. The negative health effects of these toxins on humans include brain, heart, liver, kidney and skeletal system damage.

6. Solar, wind, hydropower, geothermal and ocean energies don't spoil the planet and help decrease the emission of carbon dioxide. Moreover they are free and plentiful.
7. Google's platform displays digital versions of thousands of artwork. Many people feel more concerned by art and find it more accessible as they don't need to visit museums to have access to all kinds of art.
8. NFTs are successful because they give a new type of visibility to artists, boosting the art market. But the cryptocurrency system they rely on is a great source of energy consumption, increasing global warming.

5 Analyser une image

1. The scene takes place in a factory. In the background we can see robots working on some specific tasks. In the foreground an employee (wearing some protective clothing) is talking to the boss (wearing a white shirt) about the robots.
2. Réponse b. The caption means that robots are becoming as intelligent and demanding as humans.
3. Industrial robots were first meant to be machines. With the introduction of AI, they are more and more intelligent. Some people fear they can take some workers' jobs and **outsmart** humans, even take control. The cartoonist uses irony here to sensitise people about the rise of robots, be it dangerous or not.

> **VOCABULARY**
> **outsmart**: defeat by being more clever

6 Comprendre un article de presse

1. An NFT (Non-Fungible Token) is a unique digital file that can be traded with crypocurrencies. Some of them are sold for millions.
2. NFTs are exchanged via cryptocurrencies through blockchains. These operations consume a lot of energy because many computers go through never-ending operations. This often consumes as much as a small country. Moreover this consumption emits greenhouse gases which cause global warming.
3. They boost the art market because they are more and more trendy. People like the idea of owning a unique asset. But many people warn about the danger they represent for the environment.

7 Traduction en français

1. L'expression *known as* ne peut pas être traduite mot à mot. Pour que la traduction française soit correcte, on dira « connu sous le nom de ». Si on veut être plus concis on peut utiliser « dit ».
2. *Upside down* signifie « sens dessus dessous ». Le mot *flip* évoque l'idée de retourner, renverser quelque chose. On pourrait traduire l'expression par « chambouler ».

Voici la traduction proposée.

Un artiste numérique connu sous le nom de Beeple a chamboulé le monde de l'art en vendant chez Christie's une œuvre d'art entièrement digitale pour plus de 69 millions de dollars en mars. Mais le serveur numérique sur lequel cette œuvre d'art – appelée **NFT** – est stockée émet chaque année dans l'atmosphère plus de carbone que la plupart des petits pays. Pourquoi tout le monde est-il donc si désireux de surfer sur la tendance des NFT ?

INFO

Non-fungible token se traduirait par « jeton non fongible » mais c'est l'acronyme anglais NFT qui est utilisé en français.

OBJECTIF BAC

8 Synthèse de documents • Science and the American nation

Les titres en couleur et les puces permettent de mettre en évidence la structure du corrigé mais ils ne figureraient pas sur une copie de bac.

Introduction

How has science shaped the American nation? The documents highlight the specificity of the American spirit in this scientific crusade, insisting on the advantages brought in by science but also questioning the negative impacts science sometimes has.

Science as a backbone of the American Dream

- President Obama speaks for the American people in his 2016 final State of the Union address, when he says the "spirit of discovery is in our DNA" (C, l. 5). The USA is a land of opportunity where immigration is a great asset. Steve Jobs's amazing success couldn't have been possible if his father hadn't immigrated to the US.
- Famous American scientists are an example of the success America has achieved (C, l. 5-7). The cartoon (A) highlights the massive presence of robots in industry, originating from the two American scientists who created the first robot in the 1960s. New American innovations are always **looming**, as Obama mentioned in his speech when he said : "Let's make America the country that cures cancer once and for all" (C, l. 20).
- America is a **hive of activity** where people and businesses challenge and are challenged every day. This dynamism has been increased by worldwide competition. The Space Race during the Cold War tickled America's spirit of success.

VOCABULARY

loom: appear imminent
hive of activity: busy place

Scientific breakthroughs as assets to shape a dynamic nation

- One of the biggest scientific breakthroughs is the creation of the first **robot** in the 1960s. The rise of industrial robots and the automation of almost every field of our lives have boosted the economy of companies.
- Such innovations are **a never-ending process** because the USA has "launched next generation manufacturing hubs, and online tools that give an entrepreneur everything he or she needs to start a business" (C, l. 11-13). The growing access to the **Internet** makes everything easier. Technology both helps consumers and boosts the economy. Las Vegas CES highlights this American thirst for tech innovations. Art is also at the forefront of innovation and economic prosperity with the NFTs, digital files exchanged via cryptocurrency.
- Developing **clean energy sources** helps fight global warming. This matches both environmental and economic issues. Obama makes it clear : "Why would we want to pass up the chance for American businesses to produce and sell the energy of the future?" (C, l. 24-26).

Science as a double-edged tool endangering the nation and the planet

- Some people have always feared the over-growing presence of technology. What fiction has often depicted as **a frightening future** now appears more concrete. Robots are said to be taking our jobs. The cartoonist (A) plays on this fear robots and Artificial Intelligence could be overcoming humanity.
- Technology improvements mean **more energy consumption**. The Internet and digital files like NFTs are a great source of **digital pollution**. The system of crypto-currencies contributes "to the destruction of Earth's atmosphere" (B, l. 24-25).

> **VOCABULARY**
> **double-edged**: acting two ways

Conclusion

Therefore science is a **double-edged tool**. It makes humans better, our lives easier and it is an asset for economic growth. But some scientists think the lust for improvement should have limits. Ethics must remain at the core of any scientific breakthrough. Transhumanism and the challenge of eternal (digital) life may be the most fascinating but scary example.

(491 words)

> **CONSEIL**
> Terminez votre conclusion en évoquant un sujet qui permet d'ouvrir votre réflexion vers d'autres horizons, tout en restant dans la même thématique.

3 Every voice counts: representation and participation

In 1964, the Civil Rights Act was enforced in the USA. It outlawed discrimination and segregation based on colour, religion and sex. It also provided enhanced mechanism for voting rights and therefore a better representation for non-white citizens.

9 British legacy and Commonwealth

En bref *Many English-speaking countries have adopted parliamentary representation and the Commonwealth encapsulates this idea. To what extent do member-states of the Commonwealth share common features regarding political representation?*

I British legacy

1 English heritage

- During colonisation and "British rule", Britons had a huge impact on the territories owned by the Crown. **Colonisation** shaped the English-speaking world today and spread the British political legacy worldwide for around 500 years.
- About **370 million people speak English as their first language**. Moreover, English is by far the most commonly spoken and studied language. There are 100 **British Councils** around the world to promote the knowledge of the UK and the English language. Around 1.4 billion people speak English in the world.

2 Political legacy

- Most former British colonies use **Common Law**, known as judicial precedent (= tradition). It means that it gives weigh to former cases to judge a new one. Their legal system is based on **Habeas Corpus** emanating from the **Magna Carta** that dates back to the 13th century.

INFO
Habeas Corpus is a piece of law voted in England in 1679 that guarantees that no one can be imprisoned without being brought to a judge (and be represented) to decide the legality of the detention.

- Many former British colonies have adopted a bicameral (two-Houses parliament) regime of **parliamentary democracy**, which means that citizens elect representatives to a legislative parliament that makes the law.
- Most of English-speaking countries are based on **a two-party system**: usually a conservative party and a progressist party share elected offices alternately. Not only is it the case in the UK with the Conservative Party and the Labour Party, but also in New Zealand, Canada, Australia, USA (Republicans and Democrats), etc.

II Organisation of the Commonwealth

1 Statutes

- **The Commonwealth of Nations**, known as the Commonwealth is an international organisation which consists of 54 members. These nations are almost all former territories of the British Empire.

- Headquartered in London, the **Commonwealth** was created in 1926 and formalised in 1931 when countries started to secede from the British Empire. It was restructured though the Declaration of London in 1949 in order to establish its member states as "free and equal". The main goal was to ease the process of decolonisation.

INFO
The terms "**common**" and "**wealth**" mean to share the good that these nations have in common.

- The Head of this political association is the British Monarch, who is also the head of 16 independent countries called "dominions" (Australia, Canada...). Other members are republics (South Africa, India...) and five have different monarchs. It gathers 2.5 billion people: 1/3 of the world population.
- Today, the Commonwealth promotes democracy, human rights and the rule of law. These concepts are written in the Commonwealth Charter, which a country needs to meet to remain in the organisation.

2 Representation and participation

- Bi-lateral agreements (diplomatic representation, work permit, visa...) strengthen the ties between member states. It also gives the chance to smaller countries to have their voices heard and a stronger representation.
- Commonwealth citizens living in the UK can vote for UK parliamentary elections and local elections. British citizens who reside in a Canadian province can vote at a provincial level.

zoom

A breakthrough in politics: Habeas Corpus

- W. Hogarth portrays members of the gaols committee during a hearing of a prisoner about his dreadful living conditions. In the early 18th century, British prisons or gaols were known for brutality.
- So, in 1729, the House of Commons decided to establish a committee "to enquire into the state of gaols in this Kingdom". It was the beginning of humanitarian concerns but also the rights of defence, a tangible application of Habeas Corpus.

→ Find out more about this painting: bit.ly/PbacAMC1re_3a

William Hogarth, *The Gaols Committee of the House of Commons*, 1729.

10 Current political situations in English-speaking countries

En bref *A democracy is the political system that best represents the diversity of opinions. However, it is fragile, as it can easily be overturned by autocrats who therefore can jeopardise the voices of people. What is the state of democracy in English-speaking countries?*

I A strong democratic tradition

1 Democracies

- Democracy has been adopted by most of the English-speaking countries and the United States is said to be one of the oldest democracies in the world. Another common point shared is the three branches of government: the executive (the President or Prime Minister), the legislative (lower and upper houses) and the judicial (the different courts).

- Political pluralism whether it be federally or locally is also a strong mark of a democratic regime. In the USA, power is shared between local power (the 50 States) and the central government in Washington. In the UK, **devolution** has granted regional powers to Scotland and Wales in education, agriculture, transport... In 1997 voters chose to create a Scottish Parliament and a National Assembly for Wales.

> **KEY WORD**
> **Devolution** is the process by which a national government gives more power to a local assembly.

2 Autocracies

- Yet, there are authoritarian regimes in the English-speaking world. They are often run by one almighty president or head of state (Cameroon, Eswatini, Pakistan, Nigeria, Malaysia...). Even if there are elections, pluralism is not always respected during political campaigns. They are often marred by a high level of political violence, so the citizens are not accurately represented.

- Zimbabwe was suspended from the Commonwealth in 2002 after an election widely seen as flawed, and then withdrew in 2003. The Gambia left the organisation in 2013 and rejoined it in 2018. Fiji whose membership was suspended three times because of military coup is now back in the Commonwealth.

II Parliamentary monarchy vs. republic

1 Britain facing the young American republic

- In Britain there is no written or codified constitution: it is based on Common Law with a parliamentary or constitutional monarchy. Freed from Britain in 1783 (the end of the American War of Independence), a young republic, the

United States of America, was born with a written constitution and a presidential form a government. → FICHE 9

■ The American Constitution was signed in 1787 in Philadelphia. The aim was to reinforce the national government as states operated like independent countries. The Bill of Rights were ten amendments guaranteeing basic individual protections, such as freedom of speech and religion. They became part of the **Constitution** in 1791.

KEY WORD
A **constitution** is a set of basic laws and principles that a country is governed by.

2 Being faithful to the Crown?

■ In today's Commonwealth, some countries or territories want to cut loose from Britain to gain a better representation. This is the case for Australia and Scotland. In 1999, Australia held a referendum. One of the two questions was whether Australia should become a republic with a president elected by parliament. The "NO" polled 55% of the votes. In the latest survey, the "YES" obtained 52%.

■ Other territories held referendums such as Gibraltar and the Falklands. Yet both regions refused independence. Also, citizens from these two territories do not have the same identity claims as the Scottish do. → ZOOM

zoOm

2014: "Should Scotland be an independent country?"

■ An independence referendum was held in 2014 in Scotland. Scottish citizens were asked to answer this question "Should Scotland be an independent country?". 55.3% answered "NO" while 44.7% said "YES".

■ Only four council areas voted "YES", but they are highly populated and urban, so they represent a high density of citizens. The largest councils are rural and less populated. It shows that the number and the size of councils are not relevant. Note that citizens from the Commonwealth were entitled to vote.

→ Find out more about Scottish independence:
bit.ly/PbacAMC1re_3b

11 Representativeness of institutions and counterpowers

En bref *Most political systems are based on representative or indirect democracy. Traditional parties and the left-right divide are questioned by citizens who ask for more participation. How are citizens in democratic English-speaking countries represented?*

I Political systems

1 Presidential and parliamentary democracy

- The US political system is called presidential democracy, focusing on the election of the president. It also manifests with two chambers: the upper house (the Senate) and the lower house (the House of Representatives). The president, the chief executive, and his or her vice president are elected every four years.

- The political system in the United Kingdom, Australia and New Zealand is called parliamentary democracy. The Head of State is the British monarch, but he/she has no real power. The executive power is in the hand of the Prime Minister (PM) who has the majority of seats in the **lower house**, so the PM is not directly elected by the citizens.

INFO
In the UK, the system also manifests with **two chambers**: the upper house (the House of Lords) and the lower house (the House of Commons).

2 Representativeness and balance of powers

- These political systems guarantee, more or less, the opinion and the representation of the citizens. In the UK, the PM is not elected directly by the voters (although he/she is appointed by the Monarch) and in the USA, citizens choose their president by voting for Electoral College members (universal indirect suffrage) who then vote for the president. Both rely on a two-party system. → FICHE 9

- When presidential election is held, American citizens also make their voices heard on local referendums about subjects that affect their cities.

- Power given in an official election is limited though. In the USA, in 1787, a system of checks and balances is set up to ensure no single branch (executive, legislative or judicial) would have too much power. In the UK, the "Shadow Cabinet" (the opposition) plays this role.

II Ideological and political mutations

1 Other political power

- Political participation is not the only way to have your say. Citizens can gather in trade unions, form pressure groups or NGOs (non-governmental organisations). The AFL-CIO (the American Federation of Labor) represent more than 12 million active and retired workers.

- Direct commitment is made possible thanks to the Internet. A strong aspiration to become fully participative (direct democracy) in societal issues is expressed by cyberactivism. → FICHE 12

2 A desire to change

- Pressure on the traditional system is seen through new claims whether it be ecologist with self-sufficient communities, or the will to gain more power locally.
- Some English-speaking countries want to reach a fairer representation of citizens. 10% of Members of the House of Commons are from ethnic minority backgrounds, if this figure reflected the population, there would be about 19%.

KEY FIGURES
US Senate: 24% are **women**.
Australian Senate: 53% are women.

- The slow weakening of traditional parties has triggered the gradual appearance of third parties (UKIP in the UK, Tea Party in the USA...). The effect of the Internet on voting behaviour is a fact and paradoxically has sparked a desire for strong populist men to snatch the system. D. Trump was elected President in 2016 because he knew how to take advantage of this evolution. → FICHES 12, 14 et 16

zoOm

American civil liberties organisations

- The role of the ACLU (American Civil Liberties Union) and other associations such as the NAACP (National Association for the Advancement of Colored People) were decisive for obtaining new rights. On May 18, 1954, they obtain the Supreme Court ban segregation in public schools, as seen on the front page of the newspaper proudly showed by the mother to her girl in the footage.

- After years of protest, the Civil Rights Act was enacted in July 1964 under Democrat Lyndon Johnson's presidency. It outlaws discrimination based on race, colour, religion, sex, and later sexual orientation.

→ Find out more about the American Civil Liberties Union: bit.ly/PBacAMC1re_3c

12 Democracy 3.0

En bref *Democracy 3.0 is participatory democracy mainly aiming at brushing up traditional politics, giving more opportunities for citizens to speak out and according to its promoters a better representation thanks to online technology. However appealing, to what extent does democracy 3.0 jeopardise democracy?*

I What is democracy 3.0?

1 A new form of political participation

- Democracy 3.0 aims at erasing all kinds of intermediary between the citizens and the elected representatives. No more influence of money, lobbyists or **gerrymandering**.

> **KEY WORD**
> **Gerrymandering** means changing and manipulating the boundaries of electoral district to advantage your political party.

- There are many advantages of a liquid democracy (= democracy 3.0). Citizens can launch petition or vote online in some US States and Australia. However, problems may appear as the system may be hacked or citizens can be influenced in their households. Electronic voting is said to favour the youth voters, country citizens and the disabled.
- 2020 US presidential election turnout increased by 7.7% compared with the 2016 election thanks to nontraditional voting methods (by mail and/or before Election Day or using e-voting) but also thanks to a strong rallying of Democrat voters.

2 A digital democracy

- For the past few years social networks have had an influence on politics. Today, **cyberactivism** allows any individual or organisation to utilise social networks to support a cause. It is a new kind of political participation. Yet, is the future of civic engagement online?

> **KEY WORD**
> **Cyberactivism** is a type of activism facilitated by Internet-based communication techniques.

- However, algorithms send false emails or post biased comments to discredit the targeted candidate (e.g. Hillary Clinton in 2016). Therefore we can say that social media have emerged as a political intermediary used to assert influence and achieve political goals, which goes against the idea of a liquid democracy.
- Unethical microtargeting (ads, messages, fake news sent to voters) during US, Canadian or Nigerian political campaigns have been revealed by Canadian whistleblower Christopher Wylie. → FICHE 15

II Can democracy 3.0 be dangerous?

1 Media and influence

- Media have always influenced citizens' opinions and political participation, but it has been more significant over the past years. TV channels such as Fox News in the USA was alleged to have favoured D. Trump's candidacy.

- The use of traditional media to get information is sharply decreasing to the benefit of social networks. There is an ambiguous relationship between media, politicians and citizens. Some media or politicians give a distorted vision of reality, for example during the Brexit campaign for the "leave" or concerning the Covid-19 pandemic.

2 Threats to democracy

- All these new digital means of dealing with politics have their limits. They can be used to jeopardise democracy and therefore the representation of citizens by interfering with elections. Major democracies are facing cyberattacks from rogue countries.

- Distrust of the traditional media and institution increase the citizens' resentment. Some citizens feel they are not represented and are suspicious of the elite. They are hacktivists and spread conspiracy theories via the Net. One of the most significant groups is QAnon, a far-right cult that spreads horrific ideas on the Internet.

zoOm

Conspiracy vs. democracy

- On Jan. 6, 2021, hundreds of protesters have invaded the US Capitol, after being called on social media to barge into building. Trump's twittermania aroused white conspiracy theorists to rebel against US most significant place of democracy in their ill-fated effort to overturn the 2020 US presidential election.

- The three men on the photograph are stereotypical of hardcore Trump supporters that not only feel they have been stolen their election but also want to show their distrust in democracy. Jake Angeli, the shirtless man wearing a horned hat (like a modern Davy Crockett), is clearly playing with the camera that is shooting him.

→ Find out more about the Capitol riot: bit.ly/PbacAMC1re_3d

MÉMO VISUEL

Commonwealth, a shared legacy?

British legacy

- **British Empire** (16th century to mid-1950s) and decolonisation
- Common Law, **Habeas Corpus**, Magna Carta
- Parliamentary democracy and two-party system
- **English language** (2.3 billion speakers)

Statutes and representation

- **Commonwealth** since 1931
- 54 member-states
- Promoting **democracy**, human rights and the rule of law

REPRESENTATION

The Commonwealth

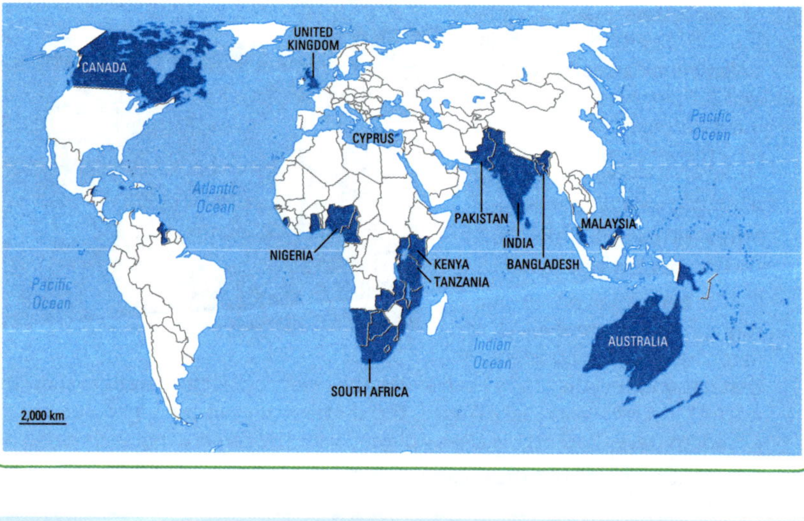

& PARTICIPATION

Various political situations

A majority of democratic regimes
- **Parliamentary** or **presidential** democracy
- Monarchy or republic
- ⚠ A few autocracies or hybrid regimes

Democratic principles and counterpowers
- **Three** equal **branches** (executive, legislative, judicial)
- Pluralism: allowing different political parties
- Possible **devolution**
- Checks and balances (USA), Shadow Cabinet (UK)

Citizens and civil society
- UK: **Common Law**, USA: **Bill of Rights**
- **Popular** sovereignty and determination
- Civil society

Martin Luther King Jr. (1929-1968)

Mutations and threats

Emancipating countries?
- Australia: will for republic?
- Scotland: breaking away from UK?

New ways of political participation and representation
- **Weakening** of traditional parties
- **Liquid democracy**
- Electronic voting and its limits
- **Cyberactivism** and whistleblowers

Dangers of digital democracy
- **Biased** media
- Distrust of peoples
- Cyberattacks, misinformation
- **Hacktivists**, conspiracy theories, QAnon

SE TESTER QUIZ

Vérifiez que vous avez bien compris les points clés des **fiches 9 à 12**.

1 British legacy and Commonwealth

→ FICHE 9

Laquelle de ces phrases est correcte ?

☐ a. The Commonwealth was created in 1936 and has nowadays 52 members.
☐ b. The Commonwealth was created in 1926 and has nowadays 54 members.
☐ c. The Commonwealth was created in 1949 and has nowadays 52 members.

2 Current political situations in English-speaking countries

→ FICHE 10

Reliez chaque pays à son système politique.

a. The United Kingdom •	• federal republic
b. The USA •	• constitutional monarchy
c. Ireland •	• parliamentary republic

3 Representativeness of institutions and counterpowers

→ FICHE 11

1. Vrai ou faux ? Cochez la case qui convient.

	V	F
a. In the UK, the Prime Minister is elected directly by citizens.	☐	☐
b. In the USA, the President is elected directly by US citizens.	☐	☐
c. Allowing NGOs and pressure groups is part of a healthy democracy.	☐	☐

2. Complétez le texte ci-dessous avec les mots qui conviennent.

In the USA, the president in elected every .... years. In fact, citizens vote for members of the .... College that then vote for the president. It is called universal .... suffrage. In the UK, citizens vote for a party whose chief is the future .... if his/her party wins the .... He/She is then .... by the Monarch.

4 Democracy 3.0

→ FICHE 12

Proposez un synonyme pour chacun des mots ou groupes de mots suivants.

a. liquid democracy: .... democracy

b. the number of people who vote in an election: ....

c. to endanger: to ....

d. a secret plan to do something that is harmful or illegal: a ....

S'ENTRAÎNER

5 Réviser le cours en 8 questions flash

→ FICHES 9 à 12

1. What are the three concepts that the Commonwealth promotes?
2. What is Habeas Corpus? When and where was it voted?
3. What are the three branches of government in democracies?
4. What is the main difference between the USA and the UK regarding their "constitution"?
5. How do you call the two chambers that sit in parliament in the USA and in the UK?
6. Why do some territories or countries want to gain independence from the UK? Give one example.
7. What are the differences between cyberactivism and hacktivism?
8. Why is the role of social media and the Internet ambivalent?

6 Analyser une carte

→ FICHE 10

Observez la carte, lisez l'explication qui l'accompagne, puis répondez aux questions (voir page suivante).

Document A Global Democracy Index

This world map from The Economist *shows the 2020 Democracy Index. The index is based on various indicators such as civil liberties, pluralism, functioning of government, political participation… It has four categories: full and flawed democracies, and hybrid and authoritarian regimes.*

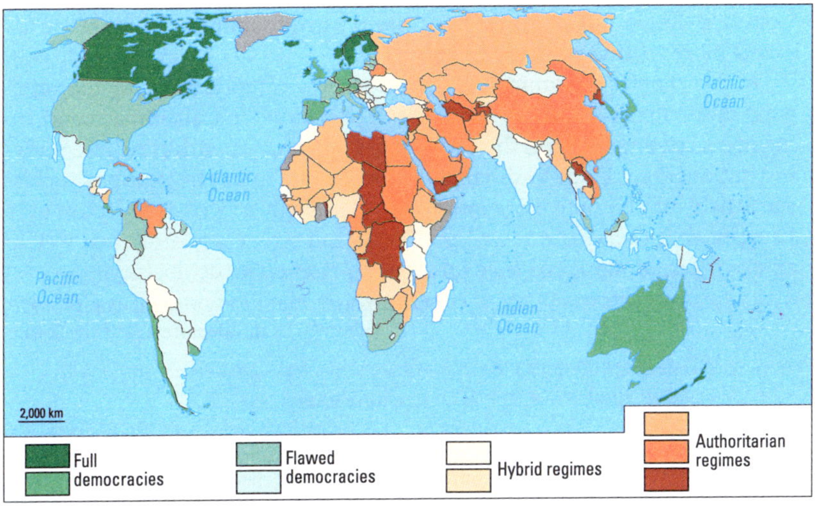

1. Focus on the four categories and colours of the Index and reformulate what each of them means.

2. Compare this map with the map the Commonwealth (page 60) and deduce the state of democracy in a few English-speaking countries. Deduce the possible role played by the Commonwealth Charter.

3. Focus on the USA. Say what is surprising.

HELP
With the help of the colours, say what you instantly understand. Show the aim of the map.

7 Comprendre un texte d'analyse politique

→ FICHE 11

Lisez le texte et répondez aux questions page suivante.

Document B Dilemmas of representation

This text is the beginning of a political analysis on representation in Australia. It was written by Marian Sawer, an Australian political specialist.

Different concepts of representation have shaped Australia's evolution as a parliamentary democracy. Currently there is renewed debate over both principles and practice of representation coinciding with a loss of faith by many citizens that their views are being represented in Australia's parliaments. Some citizens are attracted to forms of plebiscitary democracy, such as Citizen Initiated Referenda or CIR, that sideline the role of the representative and solve in this way the perceived gap between the policy preferences of policy elites and of the public. Others advocate quotas for women, reserved seats for indigenous Australians, increased representation of Australians from non-Anglo backgrounds or of those with disabilities, to make parliaments more representative.

In this chapter, I examine changing concepts of representation, the ambiguity of discursive claims of 'under-representation' and dilemmas concerning increased emphasis on the embodiment of diversity within representative institutions. I conclude by discussing how parliamentary institutions such as the Senate may become more responsive to diversity as well as reflective of it. I suggest that the Senate is well positioned to become a guardian, as well as an exemplar, of more inclusive forms of representative democracy.

Marian Sawer, *Papers on Parliament*, vol. 34, 1999,
published by the Department of the Senate.

1. Focus on the important notions of the document. Find the definition or give the notion.

Notion	Definition
representation	....
....	political system where decisions are taken by the elected representatives in a parliament
plebiscitary democracy	.... democracy in which citizens make political ....
more representative	an effort to be more .... in the representation of a group of people

2. Focus on the source and the author. Explain what makes the document special.

3. Identify the aim of the author.

8 Traduction en français

Traduisez l'article du *Guardian* de « The US Capitol… » à « and surged forward » (document C, l. 1-7).

> **CONSEIL**
> « A pro-Donald Trump mob » (l. 2-3) devra être étoffé avec un nom pour « pro- ». Aussi sera-t-il nécessaire de moduler « Minutes after the news spread » (l. 4).

OBJECTIF BAC

9 Synthèse de documents • Democracy and representation

3 h

Les deux documents A (p. 63) et B (p. 64) que vous venez d'étudier et le document qui va suivre (C) constituent le dossier à analyser pour l'épreuve de synthèse portant sur la thématique « Représentations » et plus particulièrement l'axe « Faire entendre sa voix : représentation et participation ».

LE SUJET

Prenez connaissance du dossier proposé, composé des documents A, B et C non hiérarchisés, et traitez en anglais le sujet suivant (500 mots maximum) :

Say what the documents show about the state of democracy and the political participation of citizens in English-speaking countries. Explain the importance of democratic representative institutions.

Document C Maga[1] mob's Capitol invasion makes Trump's assault on democracy literal

The US Capitol, the seat of American democracy, has been stormed by a pro-Donald Trump mob, egged on by the president in a desperate and violent effort to overturn the results of the election.

Minutes after the news spread that the vice-president had announced he would not do the president's bidding and reverse Trump's defeat to Joe Biden at the ballot box, hundreds of pro-Trump rioters broke down the barriers around the Capitol building, and surged forward. [...]

A group [of rioters] managed to make their way to the atrium of the Senate Rotunda, carrying Confederate flags. The Capitol police were outnumbered and seemed to melt away.

One female rioter was shot and later died of her injuries, according to the DC police. Three other people experienced "medical emergencies" throughout the day and died. Explosive devices were found near the offices of the Democratic National Committee and the Republican National Committee. Several police officers were also injured.

It was the most dramatic challenge to the US democratic system since the civil war and it forced the suspension of a joint session of Congress that had convened to certify the results of November's presidential election. [...]

The crowds in Washington, however, had been told by their leader that the votes against him [D. Trump] had been rigged, and told to march on the Capitol to "stand strong for the integrity of our elections" and to "save our democracy".

Trump told them to converge on Congress "peacefully and patriotically" but order broke down just minutes after he spoke.

The mob, in Make America Great Again caps, rushed up the Capitol steps, forcing the police to withdraw, firing flash-bangs and paintballs from higher balconies in an effort to keep them at bay. [...]

In the eyes of the rioters, the democratic procedures and traditions of which the US has thus far been so proud, had been transformed, by their leader's insistent oratory, into the mere trappings of betrayal.

As protesters took selfies inside the Senate chamber and offices, Trump tweeted "Remember, WE are the Party of Law & Order respect the Law and our great men and women in Blue." [...]

Biden said the violence at the Capitol "borders on sedition" and "must end now". "I call on President Trump to go on national television now, to fulfill his oath and defend the constitution and demand an end to this siege," Biden said. "It's not a protest; it's insurrection. The world is watching." [...]

Hours after his supporters had stormed the Capitol, Trump released a video telling them: "Go home, we love you, you're very special,". But he also used the video to repeat his baseless claims about the "fraudulent" vote which he lost.

At the other end of the national mall, half an hour before the Capitol was besieged, the defeated president had painted a stark picture. Those Republicans who voted to upturn the election were the patriots, and the others were "weak" and "pathetic" allowing Democrats to destroy the country. [...]

Kasey [a passer-by] said: "I think Trump's only option he really has left is to call military action into it because he has the right to do that."

Julian Borger, *The Guardian*, 7 January 2021,

1. Maga = Make America Great Again (D. Trump's slogan in 2016 presidential campaign)

▶▶▶ LA FEUILLE DE ROUTE

→ *Reportez-vous à la méthode générale de la synthèse de documents, p. 128-129.*

Étape 1 Analyser les termes du sujet

- *State of democracy :* il s'agit de « l'état de santé » démocratique d'un pays. Interrogez-vous sur la localisation des pays anglophones, leur liens géopolitiques et leur appartenance au Commonwealth.
- *Political participation of citizens :* quelles sont les résonnances de ce concept dans les documents ? Comment la représentation s'exerce-t-elle ?
- *English-speaking countries :* bien veiller à mentionner et étudier seulement des pays de l'aire anglophone notamment les États-Unis et l'Australie (docs B et C).
- *Democratic representative institutions :* les différentes institutions démocratiques sont très présentes dans les documents B et C, notamment la chambre haute. Quels rôles peut-elle avoir ?

Étape 2 Lire et analyser le corpus à la lumière de la problématique

- Document C focuses on January 6th, 2021 when pro-Trump rioters stormed the US Capitol to disrupt and prevent the Congress from formalising Joe Biden's victory as the new President of the USA.
- Connect this event (doc C) with information given by the map (doc A) and contrast them with the situation of Australia in doc B. To what extent do the documents show that there are great dangers to democracy but also show that these representative democracies may be improved?

Étape 3 Analyser et comparer l'apport de chaque document

	Uneven democracies	Democracy and participation to be strengthened and protected	Redefining democracy and representation
Doc. A Map	Democracy is not self-evident.	The USA is a "flawed democracy".	
Doc. B Political analysis		Not inclusive enough.	Proposal to the Australian government by political specialist.
Doc. C Press article	Some US citizens feel they have been stolen their election. Violent actions to make themselves heard.	The American democracy can be in danger.	Democracy (even if already representative) can be improved.

Étape 4 Construire le plan de la synthèse

I. Uneven democracies

II. Democracy to be strengthened and protected

III. Redefining democracy and representation

Étape 5 Rédiger la synthèse → CORRIGÉ p. 71

CORRIGÉS

SE TESTER QUIZ

1 British legacy and Commonwealth

Réponse b. The Commonwealth was created in 1926 and has nowadays 54 members.

2 Current political situations in English-speaking countries

a. The United Kingdom: constitutional monarchy. • b. The USA: federal republic. • c. Ireland: parliamentary republic.

INFO
The US is a federal republic because it is composed of 50 States with three levels of government: local, State and federal.

3 Representativeness of institutions and counterpowers

1. a. Faux. British citizens vote for a party whose leader will become the Prime Minister if he or she obtains the majority of seats in the House of Commons. He or she will be appointed by the Monarch.
b. Faux. American citizens vote for a representative of the chosen party (Electoral College), then the member of the Electoral College accordingly votes for the future president.
c. Vrai. There are also trade unions, associations...
2. In the USA, the president in elected every four years. In fact, citizens vote for members of the Electoral College that then vote for the president. It is called universal indirect suffrage. In the UK, citizens vote for a party whose chief is the future Prime Minister if his/her party wins the election. He/She is then appointed by the Monarch.

4 Democracy 3.0

a. liquid democracy: participative democracy.
b. the number of people who vote in an election: turnout.
c. to endanger: to jeopardise.
d. a secret plan to do something that is harmful or illegal: a conspiracy.

S'ENTRAÎNER

5 Réviser le cours en 8 questions flash

1. The Commonwealth promotes democracy, human rights and the rule of law.
2. The Habeas Corpus is a piece of law voted in England in 1679 that guarantees that no one can be imprisoned without being brought to a judge (and be represented) to decide the legality of the detention.
3. The executive (the President or Prime Minister), the legislative (lower and upper houses) and the judicial (the different courts) are the three branches of government in democracies.
4. In Britain there is no written or codified constitution: it is based on Common Law with a parliamentary or constitutional monarchy. In the USA, the Constitution is written starting with the Bill of Rights.
5. In the USA, the two chambers are the upper house (the Senate) and the lower house (the House of Representatives). In the UK, the two chambers are the upper house (the House of Lords) and the lower house (the House of Commons).
6. Some territories want to be better represented and promote their identity. For example, Scotland wanted to gain independence in 2014 (and expects another referendum in the near future).
7. A cyberactivist can defend a fair cause or a political party through the Internet, however some cyberactivists may hide their real agenda and become hacktivists. They spread rumours, fake news to harm a person or a company.

8. Social media allow direct or participative democracy, which may be seen as positive but it also jeopardises democracy because it may allow conspiracy theories and cyberattacks during campaigns to spread worldwide.

6 Analyser une image

1. There are four sets of colours from green to dark red. Each colour refers to the state of democracy in world countries. Full democracy means that powers are shared, personal liberties are respected as well as a political representation and justice for all. Flawed democracy means that there is a lack of liberties or representation. Hybrid and authoritarian regimes mean that power is in the hands of one man or a group of men, with hardly no civil liberties and no protest possible.
2. Most English-speaking countries are full or flawed democracies. It is the case in Americas, Europe and Oceania. In Africa, South Africa, Ghana and Botswana are flawed democracies. The rest of the countries have either hybrid or authoritarian regimes.
It is interesting to see that African countries that belong to the Commonwealth are either flawed or hybrid (Tanzania, Kenya). So, we can say that the Commonwealth Charter (democracy, human right and rule of law) may play a role in maintaining a democratic society in certain countries.
3. It is surprising to notice that the USA is seen as a flawed democracy while it is said to be the "greatest democracy" in the world. Problems of democratic representation, legitimacy of elections, protests against places of power show that the American democracy seems to be in decline.

INFO
Full democracy is to be found in Australia, even if document B focuses on the lack of **full representation**.

7 Comprendre un texte d'analyse politique

1.

representation	the fact that someone speaks and makes decision for you
parliamentary democracy	political system where decisions are taken by the elected representatives in a parliament
plebiscitary democracy	participative democracy in which citizens make political decisions
more representative	an effort to be more inclusive in the representation of a group of people

2. This extract comes from a governmental source. It is written in the first-person narrative: the content of the document is Marian Sawer's opinion. If it is published on the official website of the Australian parliament, it must mean that it agrees and supports her recommendation.
3. She wants to promote more representation, especially gender and ethnic minorities (here Aborigines). She wishes the Australian representation would be more inclusive than it is now.

8 Traduction en français

Le Capitole, siège de la démocratie américaine, a été pris d'assaut par une foule de partisans de Trump encouragée par le président lui-même dans un effort désespéré et violent pour annuler les résultats de l'élection.
Quelques minutes après l'annonce du refus du vice-président d'accéder à la demande du président de faire marche arrière sur la défaite de Trump au profit de Joe Biden dans les urnes, des centaines d'émeutiers partisans de Trump ont démoli les barrières protégeant le bâtiment et ont déferlé sur le Capitole.

CONSEIL
Dans la première phrase, la répétition de *US* et *American* peut alourdir la traduction. Il n'est donc pas nécessaire de préciser « des États-Unis » pour le Capitole.

OBJECTIF BAC

9 Synthèse de documents • Democracy and representation

Les titres en couleur et les puces permettent de mettre en évidence la structure du corrigé mais ils ne figureraient pas sur une copie de bac.

Introduction

Democracy is not-self-evident. It is indeed an everyday life struggle. The documents under scrutiny deal with the state of democracy in the English-speaking world but more precisely in the USA and Australia. They show that there are big dangers to democracy but also that these representative democracies can be improved.

Uneven democracies

- All three documents show **the state of democracy at some level**. The map presents the different regimes in the world categorising them, showing their democracy indexes. In her political analysis (B) Marian Sawer reflects on the improvement of representation in Australia and *The Guardian*'s article focuses on the dangers that democracy could face in the USA.
- Democracy should provide **a guarantee of civil liberties**. Yet it is not the case in quite a few English-speaking countries which are members of the Commonwealth (A) even if efforts are made by the organisation to ensure its members do so.
- Democracy is fragile, even "the greatest democracy", **the USA, is under threat**. The headline of the article sums up it all: "an assault on democracy".

Threats on democracy

- "Save our democracy" (C) was what Donald Trump said to the rioters. Saying that, it shows how ambivalent he was. **The paradox** lies in the use of the word "democracy", meaning that the new power in place is not democratic. In fact, D. Trump claimed he represented the "real" America, it is hence a new form of **undemocratic representativeness**.

■ However in C, the sole means to protest is violence ignited by former President. Ready to invade the Capitol, the rioters jeopardised democracy; therefore, one can ask: **where are the limits of acceptance of representation?** There is a crisis of representation, a **distrust** towards federal government and democratic results.
■ When Joe Biden called this event a "sedition", a need to protect elected bodies had become urgent. The words used: "mob, surged, invasion" remind us of the Civil War, also mentioned by J. Biden. Why attack the Capitol, the "National Committees"? Because they precisely embody **democratic representation**.

CONSEIL

Pensez à présenter <u>succinctement</u> les documents, et surtout à y faire référence pour illustrer vos propos.

Redefining democracy and representation

■ From the second paragraph of her analysis, Sawer uses the first pronoun which indicates her full commitment in the ideas she exposes. **A better representation in the political life** of Australia is necessary in the Senate.
■ The map shows that **the USA is a flawed democracy**, and document C illustrates this state. In fact, it has been flawed for the past four years or so. People are dedicated to combatting the rise of authoritarianism, or at least to finding way to avoid that (B).
■ "A loss of faith" (B), of democracy (A) and a gap between the elite and the public" (B, and implicitly C) should be the trigger to encourage a better, more inclusive representation and pluralism of opinions in the respect of the rule of law within a **direct democracy**.

Conclusion

Democracy is the easiest regime to overturn. It is fragile and should be strengthened by citizens who are willing to reach **a fairer representation of themselves**. As W. Churchill said: "It has been said that democracy is the worst form of government except for all those other forms that have been tried from time to time..."

(515 words)

4 Breaking the news and getting informed

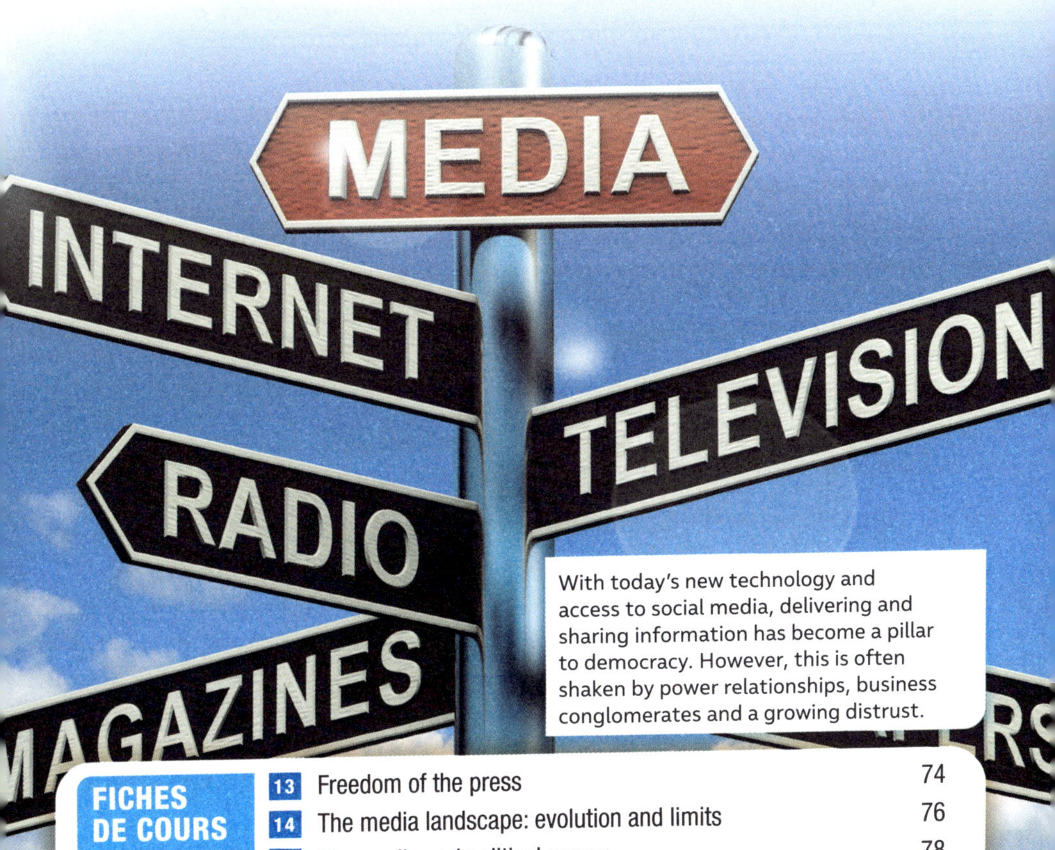

With today's new technology and access to social media, delivering and sharing information has become a pillar to democracy. However, this is often shaken by power relationships, business conglomerates and a growing distrust.

13 Freedom of the press

En bref *The first amendment to the US Constitution protects the freedom of the press, a critical element in a democracy. Not only does free media function as a watchdog against wrongdoings, but it is also a platform and a vehicle of ideas. However, in our modern world, how can we guarantee freedom of the press while limiting hate speech?*

I Barometer for a free press

1 An American principle

- The First Amendment to the US Constitution (1791) is a key component to the American system of checks and balances. It guarantees the freedom to air diverse points of view and to make governments accountable for their actions.
- For instance *The New York Times* has been involved in two historic Supreme Court cases: **New York Times Co. v. Sullivan** (1964) and the Pentagon Papers (1971).

INFO
This landmark Supreme Court ruling established that the freedom of speech protected by the First Amendment restricts the ability of American public officials to sue for defamation.

2 Challenges in the Commonwealth

- The British press appeared as early as the 16th century and the first regular daily newspaper was launched in 1702. Despite this long tradition of inquisitive press, the UK does not have any constitutional guarantee.
- Sarcasm and satires have been historical modes of expression to display criticism of the British government. A feeling of hostility and suspicion towards journalists has emerged under Boris Johnson's government, with repeated verbal attacks or ways to prevent journalists from asking questions during press conferences.
- Despite the fact that the Commonwealth Charter (2013) commits the different member countries to the free flow of information, some countries are facing challenges → FICHE 9. Media watchdogs have red-flagged India as one of "the most dangerous countries in the world".

II A vehicle of ideas

1 Are there limits to the freedom of the press?

- Freedom of the press could at times lead to fake news and the proliferation of hate speech, negationism (or denialism), xenophobic or sexist comments on different platforms, especially on the Internet.

- In the United States, such statements are covered by the First Amendment: defamation and hate speech are thus **not regulated**.
- The press's apparent **unbiased** stand is questioned by big **media owners** such as Rupert Murdoch → FICHE 14. They have the power to influence public opinion drastically, which allows for a **misrepresentation** of the truth.

2 New platforms, new rules?

- The Internet journalists face **closer scrutiny** and even repression in some authoritarian regimes. **Reporters Without Borders** defends the idea that rights granted offline should also be applied for the Internet.

> **INFO**
> **Reporters Without Borders (RWB)** is an international NGO that believes freedom of the press is a fundamental right.

- On July 19, 2021 the American DOJ (Department of Justice) adopted a policy **prohibiting the use of surveillance** on journalists. This is a huge victory for ensuring press freedom and journalists' investigative work.

zoOm

Freedom of the Press Worldwide in 2021

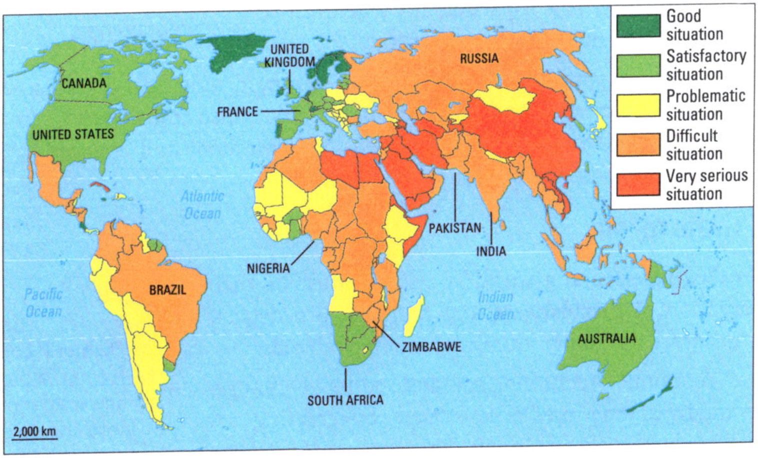

- This map – published by Reporters Without Borders every year – ranks the countries from top to bottom in their respect of the freedom of the press and the free access to information. The 2021 data collection shows a **clear deterioration of people's access to information**.
- It is surprising to see that the UK is ranked 33 and the US 44 (in light green). This map also clearly shows that some countries from the **Commonwealth** are not well ranked either: Pakistan and India (in orange) are respectively 146 and 142 out of 180, Nigeria and Zimbabwe (in orange) are 120 and 130.

→ Find out more about Reporters Without Borders: bit.ly/PbacAMC1re_4a

14 The media landscape: evolution and limits

En bref *The media landscape has evolved rapidly with the emergence of the Internet. The way people share and consume information has changed drastically, even if the media in the English-speaking world is standing strong. What are today's stakes?*

I Global media

The media commonly refers to the various means of communication providing the public opinion with facts and knowledge.

1 Public media

- In the US, the public service consists of **PBS** for television and NPR for the radio. In the UK, the BBC is the major public media service.
- The system of public media services – both in the UK and in the US – is based on a strong principle of political neutrality. This is particularly true in the US where "objectivity norms" is a core value.

> **INFO**
> **Public Broadcasting Service** is a non-profit organisation that airs programmes on TV. It compiles more than 350 local stations. PBS is often praised for the overall variety and quality of its programming.

- Public media is supposed to offer more in-depth, ideologically diverse and critical news about domestic and international affairs. It also contributes to creating a trustworthy environment where citizens feel confident and engaged in their political and democratic institutions.

2 Private media

- The English-speaking world is also famous for their combination of **broadsheets** and **tabloids**. Broadsheets are considered as quality journalism unlike tabloids.
- The economic, technological and political changes have modified the media landscape by creating big conglomerates such as Google, Facebook or Australian Rupert Murdoch's news empire. → ZOOM

> **INFO**
> The names **"broadsheet"** and **"tabloid"** come from the format: a broadsheet is a newspaper printed on large sheets of paper; a tabloid is printed on smaller sheets of paper.

II The advent of the Internet

1 Hybrid forms of information

- The recent evolution has had major financial consequences such as the drastic downsizing of reporters. Readership and the circulation of the printed press has declined steadily in favour of online news.

■ Indeed, online only newspapers (*HuffPost*, *Slate*...) have appeared and Google and Facebook – which are not "media companies" – contribute to the flow of information.

■ Participatory journalism has developed in recent years. It consists of ordinary citizens participating in the process of collecting and sharing first-hand information. Citizens share videos on YouTube or other private channels or blogs. These non-professional journalists blur the definition of journalism itself.

2 | Information-filtering system

■ As e-commerce and digital advertising are developing along with social media and online services, recommendation systems have become unavoidable.

■ This can be seen as a tool to help users not to be overwhelmed by the flow of information, to target information relevant to you. Users are then exposed to a small amount of information and can navigate it with more care.

■ However, users are also subjected to a narrower amount and an already oriented and biased information. These algorithms may then feed the growing divide within the nation and trigger more violence and conflicts. → FICHE 16

zoOm

Rupert Murdoch's empire

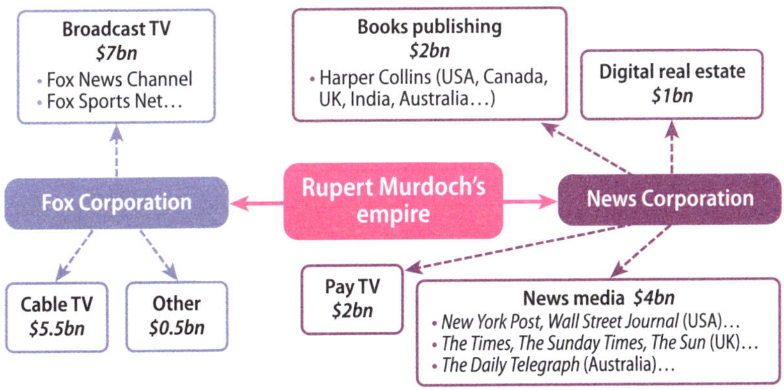

■ Rupert Murdoch is an Australian-born American media tycoon. His vast $22bn network includes tabloids and quality journalism, TV programmes, movie production, edition, etc.

■ His connection in Australian, British, American media can be seen as a threat to democracy as his media outlet can broadcast his personal views at the international level.

→ Find out more about Rupert Murdoch: bit.ly/PbacAMC1re_4b

15 The media and political power

En bref *The media helps people have a more accurate representation of the political, economic, social and diplomatic stakes in our world. Recently, they have gained more and more power. Often called the "fourth power" or "fourth estate", to what extent is the media a balancing power in democracies?*

I Political affiliation

1 Media, vehicle of ideas?

- Contrary to the US, Canada or Ireland, the UK media landscape has always maintained a strong political partisanship. The concept of "political parallelism" reflects the alignment of the British press with political parties and ideologies.
- People's assessment of the accuracy of news has dropped dramatically. A majority of Americans for instance believe that news stories are often inaccurate and that news organisations display political bias. To that effect, some research have shown that exposure to Fox News may increase Republican vote shares significantly.
- Since the 1990s, powerful TV programmes and **newspaper headlines** have had the ability to influence public opinion and to weigh in the results of elections. The media has thus become a tool for political propaganda.

INFO
"It's The Sun Wot Won It": this catchphrase was the headline of the tabloid on election day in 1992 in the UK. This is often cited in debates over the influence of the media in politics.

2 Spin doctors

- **Spin doctors** are counsellors or strategists who focus on the public relations of political figures. For instance, they organise press conferences, TV appearances, deal with the media image of politicians and manage crises.

INFO
The TV show *Scandal* starring Kerry Washington focuses on Olivia Pope, a **spin doctor** who manages different crises and secrets of politicians and toys with the way a story is told.

- While some tactics are obvious, spin doctors are also deploying more cynical tactics in order to control and influence the way the media share the information. Those tactics include leaking information, freezing some journalists out, disclosing damaging information on opponents, etc.

II Counter-power

1 Investigative journalism

- The anglo-saxon tradition of investigative journalism has revealed many scandals over the years concerning corruption, crimes or fraud. The McCarthy witch hunt (1950s), the Pentagon Papers (1971) →ZOOM, the Watergate (1972-1974) were all revealed thanks to investigative journalists.
- In 2013 *The Guardian* and *The Washington Post* won the Pulitzer Prize after publishing their story on NSA surveillance activity thanks to Edward Snowden. Seen by some as a **whistleblower**, Snowden shared inside secret intel to journalists.

KEY WORD

A **whistleblower** is a person who publicly shares intel on governments' or companies' activities in order to shed light on their wrongdoings.

2 Data journalism and new Internet opportunities

- Founded in 2006 by Julian Assange, Wikileaks has already published more than ten million documents and functions as a watchdog against frauds, corruption or scandals done by politicians and important public figures. Julian Assange is being prosecuted in the US for sharing confidential documents about the US army operations in Iraq and Afghanistan.
- Data journalism is based on collecting data to uncover stories and functions as a watchdog as it aims at scrutinising the world and the news with a new lens, based on information that would be very difficult to get otherwise. Thanks to data-driven journalists, many fiscal frauds were uncovered at the international level.

zoOm

Pentagon Papers

- In this 2017 movie, Steven Spielberg portrayed Katharine Graham – first female publisher of a major American newspaper – and Ben Bradlee – assistant editor of *The Washington Post* – in their race to unveil the "Pentagon Papers", a scandal about US cover-up operations during the Vietnam war.
- Both *The New York Times* and *The Washington Post* were competing for the release of this classified information. Both newspapers were charged but they pleaded the First Amendment in front of the Supreme Court who sided with them.

→ Watch the movie trailer: bit.ly/PbacAMC1re_4c

16 What's true?

En bref *With the proliferation of different means of communication, especially with the advent of the Internet, fake news have spread. Public opinion is more sceptical about news reports as they feel manipulated by biased information or conspiracy. How harmful are fake news in English-speaking democracies?*

I Influencing business & politics

1 Clickbait

- Clickbaits are fabricated stories to push people to click and raise the advertising revenue. Famous sites such as BuzzFeed are the perfect example of clickbait with their sensationalistic vague headline writing.
- If these headlines could be applied to news, it is mostly related to celebrities, as if this was the modern version of tabloids. Indeed, the sites are more interested in getting clicks (hence the name) rather than producing quality content.

2 Misinformation

- While **fake news** are often associated to social networks, only the platform is new as propaganda has always existed in the media landscape.

> **KEY WORD**
> **Fake news** is the deliberate disinformation for a profit. Most often, we associate it to a political hoax usually meant to influence people's opinion on candidates.

- Fake news relies on provocative headlines and toys with people's emotions. Most often, fake news trigger negative feelings such as outrage, anger or shock. → FICHE 12
- The main reason for creating fake news is angering people against a political opponent. This political **propaganda** aims at polarising people's opinions, promoting extremism and hate speech and reducing trust in democracy.

> **KEY WORD**
> **Propaganda** is the use of the media and any means of communication to convey a message and influence people's opinion.

3 Conspiracy theories

- Conspiracy theories have long existed and people who believe in them often blame the media for covering up the truth.
- QAnon is a movement that defends several conspiracy theories. It has dealt with issues such as Black Lives Matter, the presidential election, and the pandemic. Many of its followers participated in the deadly Capitol riot in January 2021.

II Fighting fake news

1 Social networks' responsibility

- What is being done about fake news? In the past years, social media companies have been in the spotlight. They have been pinpointed as responsible for the fast-spreading of fake news and for their lack of reactivity about it.
- The BBC and other quality papers online have created a new section to counter any fake news in order to educate their readers and provide them with accurate information. Fact-checking has been put in place by most quality newspapers and media.

2 Governments' responsibility

- Trump used the term "fake news" undiscerningly during his term in order to denigrate any media that did not favour or side with him. He is responsible for this blurred line between opinion and information.
- Considering the rapid-scale development of fake news in recent years, governments are starting to recognise the necessity to fight it by imposing regulations or trying to debunk fake stories.
- However, the Covid-19 pandemic has unleashed a flood of misinformation. Spreading misinformation is now a criminal violation in some countries. In South Africa for instance, a new law passed in March 2020 punishes whoever spreads fake news on the pandemic up to 6 months of prison.

zoOm

Hoax, fake news and conspiracy theories

CDP HOME OPINION POLITICS U.S. VIDEO WORLD

5353 BREAKING NEWS I PUBLISHED: 7:52 PM 8 NOV 2016 I UPDATED: 9:50 PM 6 DEC 2017

Obama Says Illegal Voters In 2016 Won't Be Investigated, Hillary Announces Amnesty For All Illegals After Election

by Alex Cooper 5353 SHARES

SHARE ON FACEBOOK SHARE ON TWITTER

NOW ON CDP

- This headline (published in an online conspiracy-theorist media, the *Conservative Daily Post*, during the 2016 presidential campaign) is an example of political propaganda and how the phrasing of headlines can influence our perception. The fear created by the headline aims at boosting votes for Republicans.

→ Find out more about fake news: bit.ly/PbacAMC1re_4d

MÉMO VISUEL

The media: a key element of democracy

Freedom of the press

- **1st Amendment** to the US Constitution
- A **watchdog** against wrongdoings
- A vehicle of **ideas**
- Attacks against the media = **threats** to democracy
- **Hate speech**

An evolving media landscape

- **Public** vs. **private** media
- **Broadsheets** vs. **tabloids**
- Social media and the advent of the **Internet**
- **Participatory journalism**
- Recommendation system
- Risk of misinformation

BREAKING
AND GETTING

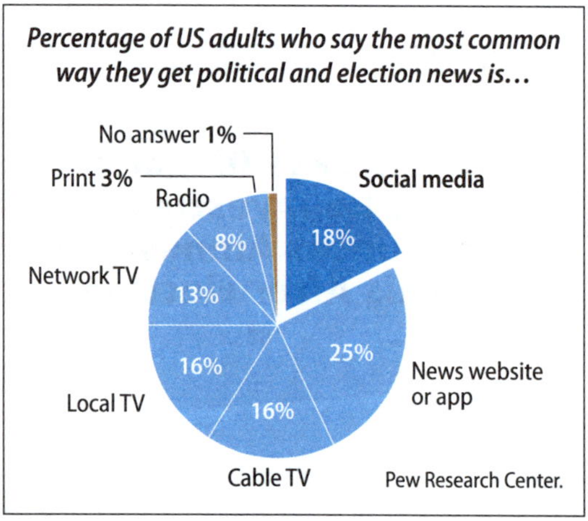

THE NEWS INFORMED

The media's influence in politics

The media at the service of political power

- Political **bias** and political **parallelism**
- Impact of media in **elections**
- **Spin doctors** (counsellors in public relations)

Are the media a counterpower?

- **Investigative** journalism and data-driven journalism
- Uncover **scandals**
- **Whistleblowers** and Wikileaks

Julian Assange

Fake news and media literacy

Influencing business and politics

- Misinformation, disinformation or fake news = **propaganda**
- **Provocative** headlines
- Clickbaits

Fighting fake news?

- **Social networks** and **government**'s responsibility
- **Fake news** as a criminal offense = dangers and potential abuse of power
- **Fact checking**

SE TESTER QUIZ

Vérifiez que vous avez bien compris les points clés des **fiches 13 à 16**.

1 Understanding the press

→ FICHES 13 et 14

1. Reliez les éléments de chaque colonne comme il convient.

a. The United Kingdom •	• Charter •	• 1791
b. The United States •	• no constitutional document •	• 2013
c. The Commonwealth •	• First Amendment •	• none

2. Vrai ou faux ? Cochez la case qui convient.

	V	F
a. Public media tend to follow political partisanship.	☐	☐
b. Participatory journalism involves politicians in the media landscape.	☐	☐
c. The development of the Internet created more jobs for journalists.	☐	☐

2 The media and political power

→ FICHE 15

1. Cochez la ou les cases qui conviennent

What are spin doctors in charge of?

☐ a. organising press conferences
☐ b. dealing with the media image of a politician
☐ c. drafting bills on freedom of speech

2. Trouvez la définition qui correspond aux mots suivants.

a. whistleblower : ....
b. data-driven journalism : ....
c. political parallelism : ....

3 What's true?

→ FICHE 16

1. Complétez le texte ci-dessous avec les mots qui conviennent.

Fake news can have an influence on both business and .... They aim at .... people's opinions to create divisions. This whole process reduces trust in the .... process and encourages citizens to .... their source.

2. Cochez la ou les cases qui conviennent.

What has been done to counter the spread of fake news?

☐ a. Social media have reacted and created fact-checking options.
☐ b. Trump has apologised.
☐ c. Regulations have been created to debunk fake stories.

S'ENTRAÎNER

4 Réviser le cours en 8 questions flash

→ FICHES 13 à 16

1. What is the main difference between the US and the UK in terms of freedom of the press?
2. Quote two reasons why there is an increased presence of hate speech in the US.
3. Why is "political neutrality" in the media important in a democracy?
4. What are the new types of media that appeared with the Internet?
5. What kind of role have social networks played in the media landscape?
6. Why can we say the media is a "fourth power"?
7. What is the aim of fake news?
8. What is being done to fight fake news?

5 Analyser un dessin de presse

→ FICHE 13

Observez le dessin et répondez aux questions.

Document A

Victor Ndula, 2017.

1. Describe the cartoon: where does the light come from and what is it lighting?
2. What title would you give this cartoon? Justify your answer.
3. What is the intent of the cartoonist? What is he denouncing and how is he doing it?

HELP
- Make sure you make a detailed description of the cartoon before answering in order to not misinterpret the message.
- Look at the source, title, pay attention to colours, contrasts, proportions and positions of the different elements.

6 Comprendre un graphique

→ FICHE 15

Observez le graphique et répondez aux questions.

Document B Social media influence on politics

The Pew Research Center is a survey company. In July 2020, it published an article revealing that "most Americans say social media has too much power, influence in politics"

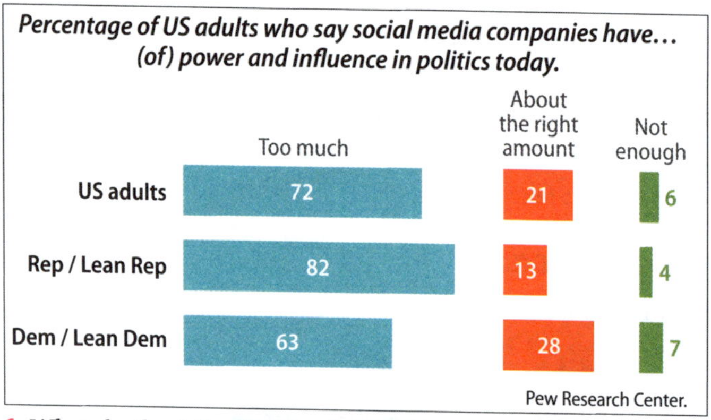

1. What do the following numbers correspond to: 72, 4, 28?
2. Compare Republicans' and Democrats' views on social media.

7 Comprendre une citation

→ FICHE 14

Lisez le texte et répondez aux questions.

Document C

The Media are corporations so… It's the concentrations of private power which have an enormous, not total control, but enormous influence over Congress and the White House and that's increasing sharply with sharp concentration of private power and escalating cost of elections and so on.

Noam Chomsky[1], interview with Laura Flanders, May 4, 2012, www.alternet.org.

1. Noam Chomsky (b. 1928) is a major American figure in linguistics and mass media studies.

1. What is the link between media and corporations?
2. Explain the warning Noam Chomsky is sending about the power of the media.

8 Traduction en français

Répondez aux questions préparatoires, puis traduisez l'article du *Rutgers Today* de « How did that deregulation… » à « news makers alike » (document D, l. 21-30).

1. Lisez la question posée par Lisa Intrabartola. Quelle est sa structure et quel est le temps employé ?

2. Comment traduiriez-vous « siloed media » (l. 27) ?

CONSEIL
Repérez l'image dégagée par le terme « **siloed** » puis étoffez-la pour trouver une image similaire en français.

OBJECTIF BAC

9 Synthèse de documents • Balance of power

3 h

Les deux documents A (p. 85) et C (p. 86) que vous venez d'étudier et le document qui va suivre (D) constituent le dossier à analyser pour l'épreuve de synthèse portant sur la thématique « Représentation » et plus particulièrement l'axe « Informer, s'informer ».

LE SUJET

Prenez connaissance du dossier proposé, composé des documents A, C et D non hiérarchisés, et traitez en anglais le sujet suivant (500 mots maximum) :

Taking into account their specificities, show how the three documents illustrate reciprocal influence and power between the media and politics.

Document D How Trump Shaped the Media

Lisa Intrabartola interviews Khadijah Costley-White, an assistant professor of journalism and media studies at Rutgers University (New Brunswick) about how the Trump presidency affected an already weak deregulated media landscape.

[…] Four years after outgoing President Donald Trump and right-wing media outlets began calling mainstream media the enemy of the people, millions of Americans question the validity of the news they are watching and reading. […]

Donald Trump worked to discredit journalists throughout his presidency, labeling the mainstream media biased. […] What are the consequences of his actions?

The right has always complained the media is biased against them, even before Trump got into office. At their best, journalists imagine themselves as the fourth estate, providing checks and balances for those in power. It is the journalist's responsibility to inform the public so they can go into a voting booth and make decisions as a nation. Trump and his encouragement of retributive[1] violence towards perceived opponents has made it more difficult for reporters to do their jobs and show up at events out of fear for their safety.

[...] What changed?

For a long time, TV news was not seen as a marketable or a profitable industry. [...] When broadcasters started realizing they could make money off TV news, we saw a shift in programming. [...] Then came the Telecommunications Act in 1996, which Bill Clinton signed, allowing media monopolies and conglomerates to grow massively, reducing the control of the media to a few select people. Soon after that Fox News was born.

How did that deregulation foster[2] the spread of disinformation [...] during the Trump administration?

Over the last several decades, producers of broadcast news became much more interested in serving a wealthy audience who could purchase things, shifting the notion of the audience and the delivered content. Being privately owned and controlled by billionaires also changed the news landscape – pushing back science, more siloed[3] media, less ethics or restrictions and the continued circulation of fake news and conspiracy theories confirmed biases many already had. All of this helped Trump use the media to his own advantage to manipulate conservatives and news makers alike.

President Obama was the first president to effectively harness[4] the power of social media. Trump is the first president to use it to bypass[5] the media and communicate directly with his base. How has that shaped media coverage of the White House?

So through social media, high-profile folks get to manage their brand without talking with journalists who will make them answer questions. The result is that the press feels like they have to fight for access and are more likely to frame their coverage in ways that give them access instead of ways that help the public. That's why Trump losing Twitter is a huge hit.

I think in the past, presidents have done their best to put out accurate information because they believe putting out clear lies would undermine their credibility and political career. Trump's support was cultivated around his brand – white supremacy, wealth and greed – so as long as he stayed loyal to his brand, his accuracy wasn't so important to his supporters.

[...] Are regulations the answer?

I think more regulation is better. There needs to be a truly public journalism source. In the UK you have the BBC, which is primarily government funded, so they have more freedom from advertisers. We have PBS and NPR, but they get very little public funding. They are very much beholden to the taste of their sponsors and audience, which is largely white and middle class. I think the other solution is appointing a FCC[6] that once again believes the public interest should be at the forefront of communication policy rather than commercial interests and profits. [...]

Rutgers University / Rutgers Today, January 19, 2021, D.R.

1. retributive: vengeful **2.** foster: encourage **3.** siloed: stored **4.** harness: exploit **5.** bypass: go around **6.** FCC (Federal Communications Commission) is in charge of communications law, regulations and technological innovation.

▶▶▶ LA FEUILLE DE ROUTE

→ *Reportez-vous à la méthode générale de la synthèse de documents, p. 128-129.*

Étape 1 Analyser les termes du sujet

- *Reciprocal influence :* influence des médias sur la politique, influence des politiciens sur les médias, système de freins et contrepoids.
- *Power :* les médias comme contre-pouvoir, surveillance des abus et fraudes.
- *Media and politics :* médias, système d'information, neutralité, alignement politique, démocratie, liberté de la presse.

Étape 2 Lire et analyser le corpus à la lumière de la problématique

- Problématique : *to what extent is the system of checks and balances working in the relationship between media and politics?*
- Repérer les différentes formes d'influence évoquées dans les documents.
- Listez les liens entre les médias et la politique afin de construire un plan.

Étape 3 Analyser et comparer l'apport de chaque document

Les documents distinguent trois types de liens entre les médias et la politique.

	The media influence politicians	Deregulation	Political manipulation of the media
Doc. A Cartoon	function as a watchdog against wrongdoings		
Doc. C Quote	influence of the media in politics	corporations create a lack of neutrality	
Doc. D Text	• the media seen as the enemy because they have revealing powers • function as informer • historical / traditional role of the press	• change in how the audience is perceived • conglomerate of private owners • need for regulations • political alignment of journalists with politicians • 1996 Clinton law = turning point • disinformation = help the Trump administration	• opposing Obama and Trump on how they handle the media • Trump bypassing media • use of social media for a direct connection with his base

Étape 4 Construire le plan de la synthèse

I. A watchdog against wrongdoings

II. Deregulation leads to disinformation

III. Political manipulation

Étape 5 Rédiger la synthèse → CORRIGÉ p. 93

CORRIGÉS

SE TESTER QUIZ

1 Understanding the press

1. a. The UK – no constitutional document – none • b. The US – First Amendment – 1791 • c. The Commonwealth – Charter – 2013

2. a. Faux. Public media are subject to political neutrality and should not display political affiliations or **bias**.

> **VOCABULARY**
> **bias**: a particular inclination, siding with a particular opinion

b. Faux. Participatory journalism involves ordinary citizens sharing information through videos, blogs, etc.

c. Faux. The Internet created a revolution in journalism and newspapers agencies had to downsize their staff drastically.

2 The media and political power

1. Réponses a et b. A spin doctor is in charge of organising press conferences, speeches, benefits and dealing with the image a politician has in the media.

> **CONSEIL**
> Lisez attentivement les questions afin de trouver la bonne réponse. Les détails comme les dates, les noms propres sont des éléments qu'il ne faut pas confondre pour consolider son propos.

2. a. Whistleblower: a concerned citizen who displays secret intel to uncover government or business operations.

b. Data-driven journalism: investigative journalism based on data collection to uncover fraud, fiscal evasion, etc.

c. Political parallelism: alignment of a newspaper with a political party or line of thoughts.

3 What's true?

1. Fake news can have an influence on both business and politics. They aim at polarising / opposing people's opinions to create divisions. This whole process reduces trust in the democratic process and encourages citizens to fact-check their source.

2. Réponse c. For instance, in South Africa new regulations have been voted.

S'ENTRAÎNER

4 Réviser le cours en 8 questions flash

1. The US guarantee freedom of the press in their Constitution, thanks to the First Amendment (1791), while the UK has no constitutional document. However, the UK has a longer history of journalism with a tolerated sarcasm.
2. The first reason is that the First Amendment protects all types of speech, including hate speech. The second reason is that social networks have made access to these types of discourse easy, instantaneous and wide range.
3. "Political neutrality" is the absence of partisanship for one political party. Public media are required to be neutral and they thus provide better-quality information which helps the democratic system.
4. With the advent of the Internet, social media have appeared. They play a part in sharing information. In addition, native online media (companies born and grown entirely online) have generated competition with old media sources.
5. Even though social networks are "tech companies", they play a part in sharing information and influencing public opinion. It has also become a platform for politicians to express their ideas faster.
6. The media functions as a watchdog because thanks to investigative journalism, politicians are under **scrutiny**. Journalists **unveil** scandals, making it a part of the "checks and balances" of power.

VOCABULARY
- **scrutiny**: a careful examination or investigation
- **to unveil**: to disclose, to reveal

7. Fake news aims at deliberately misinforming the public. In politics, it is a way to counter opponents and create outrage or negative feelings in order to manipulate people's opinion.
8. Both big tech companies and governments are now trying to counter fake news by implementing laws and regulations on their platforms. Media companies have added fake news checks on their websites.

5 Analyser un dessin de presse

1. In the spotlight, we can see a man in a suit with his right hand in a jar. Some bills are laying on the floor. The newspaper at the top is providing the light as if it was a lamp. The rest of the cartoon is dark, which symbolises secrecy.
2. The cartoon could be entitled: caught red-handed because the newspaper is revealing a scandal.
3. The cartoonist aims at showing the power newspapers have in uncovering the truth about fraud performed by a man who could be a politician or a businessman. He is criticising how some people abuse power and defending the role of the press as a counter-power.

CONSEIL
Recherchez la portée politique et le message du dessinateur : il y a généralement un aspect sarcastique, humoristique ou ironique dans un dessin de presse.

6 Comprendre un graphique

1. **72** is the percentage of American adults who think social media have too much power and influence in politics. **4** is the percentage of conservatives who think social media don't have enough power and influence in politics. **28** is the percentage of Democrats who think social media have the right amount of power in politics.
2. There is **a clear divide between Republicans and Democrats**. The survey shows that 82% of Republicans feel social media have too much power in politics whereas Democrats are only 63%. The percentage of Republicans is higher than average by 10 points, while Democrats are less likely than average to believe that social media have too much power in politics.

7 Comprendre une citation

1. Noam Chomsky insists on media being corporations, which means that they are businesses which are looking for **profit** and are not only interested in their original function, to inform.
2. Noam Chomsky is **warning the public opinion** about the power of the media as they can influence politics, the way people vote or understand a law for instance. He is also pointing out that, as corporations, media companies can also have a financial impact on elections because they can support and help finance campaigns.

CONSEIL
Une citation étant courte, il faut faire attention à tous les mots et aux différents sens possibles pour en comprendre le message.

8 Traduction en français

1. La question est composée d'un mot interrogatif (*how*) puis de l'inversion auxiliaire – sujet – verbe. La question est posée au prétérit (*did*).
2. Un silo est un grand container pour les céréales, il permet de stocker la récolte. *Siloed* peut se traduire dans un premier temps par « stocké », mais ce terme implique que ces informations ne sont pas partagées, « détenu » ou « retenu » seraient donc plus approprié.

Voici la traduction proposée.

De quelle manière cette dérégulation a-t-elle encouragé la propagation de la désinformation pendant le mandat de Trump ?

— Ces dernières décennies, les producteurs d'émissions d'actualité ont de plus en plus cherché à satisfaire un public aisé qui pouvait acheter des produits, modifiant la notion même d'audience et du contenu rendu. Le fait d'être détenus et contrôlés par des millionnaires du secteur privé a aussi changé le paysage médiatique. Le rejet de la science, la concentration des médias, l'affaiblissement de l'éthique et des restrictions, ainsi que la circulation incessante d'intox et de théories du complot ont confirmé les penchants que beaucoup avaient déjà. Tout cela a aidé Trump à utiliser les médias à son avantage afin de manipuler aussi bien les conservateurs que les journalistes.

OBJECTIF BAC

9 Synthèse de documents • Balance of power

Les titres en couleur et les puces permettent de mettre en évidence la structure du corrigé mais ils ne figureraient pas sur une copie de bac.

Introduction

Misinformation, disinformation, fake news... We live in a world where news - any kind - travels fast and can have a huge impact on our politics. The three documents are toying with the system of checks and balances at work in the relationship between media and politics and how one can influence the other and vice versa.

CONSEIL

Assurez-vous que votre synthèse prend en compte TOUS les documents du corpus. Votre plan doit comparer et contraster les documents tout au long du développement. Ne faites surtout pas de listing !

A watchdog against wrongdoings

- The notion of power is central to the three documents. Often called "the fourth power", the media participates in checking any abuse on the part of politicians and influences politics and policies (C).
- Politicians should be accountable for their actions and journalists have a central role in democracies to keep them in line (D). The historical function of newspapers is to inform the public so they could form their opinion before voting.
- The cartoon (A) clearly illustrates this function. The newspaper literally shed lights on a man caught red-handed with bills flying over him.

Deregulation leads to disinformation

- In recent years though, this power has been weakened by the conglomerates and news empire rendered possible by the 1996 Telecommunications Act (C & D). Noam Chomsky implies that TV programmes have become advertising support and the audience a commercial target, which has enabled offensive discourse to permeate.
- Political alignment has become more obvious and financial profit the aim of these broadcast news producers and owners (C & D). The interview states that news and media became the target of politicians and mainstream media lost credibility.
- Yet, disinformation has disastrous effects in a democracy, which is what Noam Chomsky and Khadijah Costley-White are denouncing (D: **"pushing back science, siloed media, less ethics"**). Both insinuate that privately owned media are more about political opinions and alignment of owners with a party.

CONSEIL

Vos citations doivent être courtes et précises afin de justifier votre argument de manière efficace. N'oubliez pas d'expliquer la citation ou de la lier à un argument. La citation vous permettra de rester proche des documents et d'éviter de faire une dissertation. Cela ancrera vos arguments dans le dossier présenté.

Political manipulation

■ Deregulation has led to a reversal of roles where politicians impact journalists. The title of the article (D) "How Trump Shaped the Media" shows the opposite vision of the cartoon (A) as it suggests that Trump manipulated the media to his advantage.

■ The relationship between politicians and the media has evolved, partly because of social media. Obama is the first president to "harness" them while Trump is the first to have used them to "bypass" the regular media. Social media gave direct access to the presidents' branding (D).

■ Khadijah Copley-White claims that Trump's dealing with the media is a new turning point as, unlike his predecessors, he did not care about accuracy of information. With Trump and his direct access to his base through social media, he broke the fourth power's main function.

■ However, as a response to Trump's behaviour some media have reinforced their function as watchdog even more (*The New York Times* or the BBC) by creating "fact-check" sections.

Conclusion

The balance of power between media and politics has changed. Despite a still strong influence, the changes in the media landscape have redefined the relationship. It seems that the media went from being a watchdog against wrongdoings, a guarantee in democracies to a profitable business support for politicians. Fortunately, regulations could balance this power relationship.

(457 words)

5 Representing the world, representing oneself

This still from the 2018 Hollywood blockbuster *Black Panther* raises key questions about identity and (re)thinking the past, proving the impact soft powers have in portraying one's society and spreading cultural values.

17 Self-portrait: a distorting mirror?

En bref *Nations shape their image through the promotion of their culture around the world. From American blockbusters promoting American values or the performances of Irish dancing shows worldwide to the British film industry with its harsh social criticism, to what extent can a nation portray itself through art?*

I Portraying a positive image

1 Patriotism in Hollywood

- American culture is a major force of globalisation. The American film industry dominates the market place and provides a means of promoting American points of view and values: personal achievement, liberty, self-government, individualism, unity and the pursuit of happiness.
- Blockbusters largely toy with an over-the-top positive image of US supremacy and international power. The best examples are the ***Independence Day*** type of movies.
- Similarly, blockbusters such as Marvel movies or war movies display extreme American patriotic values and portray the US and the citizens as leaders and saviours of the world.

> **INFO**
> ***Independence Day*** is a Roland Emmerich 1996 sci-fi movie telling the story of how the US manages to save the world from an alien invasion. There was a sequel 20 years later in 2016.

- What is at stake here is the American cultural imperialism, the dominance of American culture at the international level. It perpetuates an image of superiority in the military, social and political fields.

2 Bollywood & Co.

- At a lesser level, other English-speaking countries have managed to promote their cultural specificity and make it a strength. The billion-dollar industry of Bollywood (India) is an example of a parallel display of positivity through colourful dancing and musicals.
- Irish culture developed thanks to its diaspora around the world. The Irish dancing troupes perform all over the world, promoting traditional music and folklore.
- St Patrick's Day is celebrated in Ireland and in many countries that have welcomed the Irish diaspora, spreading Irish culture and origins through parades (in New York or Boston, the St Patrick's Day parade started in 1762), traditional food and drinks and celebrations.

II Self-deprecation

1 Social realism

- Opposite the pro-American Hollywood industry, some British films tend to promote a darker image of their nation and use self-deprecation to point out the flaws of their society.
- Ken Loach's films, as many British films, focus on social issues in order to shed light on the dysfunctions of British society.

INFO
Ken Loach is famous for dealing with poverty, workers' rights, and multiculturalism. His social vision was rewarded many times. He received the Palme d'Or at the Cannes festival for *I, Daniel Blake* in 2016 for instance.

- Street art is another form of art that tends to criticise and denounce social or environmental issues. Banksy is an anonymous thought-provoking street artist whose focus is on our consumer society and its bad consequences on social relations and the environment.

2 Political criticism

- In English-speaking African countries, and in South Africa in particular, literature is a means to convey political criticism of dictatorships in a post-colonial era, a way to give voice to the formerly oppressed people and to debunk the "single story" as Chimamanda Ngozi Adichie would say in her TedTalk. Authors such as J.M. Coetzee or Nadine Gordimer also provide auto-portrays of Apartheid or post-Apartheid South Africa. → FICHE 18
- The international prizes they have won has put South Africa in the spotlight and contributed to a rather negative image of the country, unveiling the deeply-rooted racism that existed.

zoOm

Billy Elliot, the musical

- In this British film turned into a Broadway musical, a young boy joins a dance school and starts dreaming about becoming a dancer. However, coming from a working-class background (his father is a miner), he will have to overcome obstacles to reach his dream.
- The musical is also set in a specific period of turmoil in England where miners are striking against Margaret Thatcher's government and policies.

→ Watch the trailer of the musical: bit.ly/PbacAMC1re_5a

18 National discourse, identity and communities

En bref *The debate over the renaming or removal of statues celebrating an offensive past has raised many tensions in English-speaking countries. With Black Lives Matter, or the increasing focus on indigenous history one may question the balance between national history and how communities react to this discourse.*

I Collective memory

1 Building a national narrative

- History books are filled with dates, figures, maps that appear at first as objective data. This collective data is the basis of a nation that tries to unite its people around the same core values.
- However, a national narrative is biased and the way history is told always promotes a dominant mainstream vision. → FICHE 17 When history is told by the dominant white male society, accuracy and diversity are lost. Minorities have fought long and hard to have their perspective included.
- Textbooks across the US for instance cover the same themes (slavery, the Civil Rights Movement, etc.) but with blatant differences in the way they are presented or **annotated**. History is thus a political process.

INFO
In 2020, *The New York Times* analysed a textbook used both in California and Texas to discover that political divide shapes the way **history books** are edited and the way students learn about it.

2 A contested official memory

- No wonder then that minorities have contested the official history of the different English-speaking countries as it eclipses experiences of the dominated communities, the official collective memory becomes a source of contention.
- Recently, around the world, minorities are reclaiming their past and their visibility in history. In the wake of the international Black Lives Matter movement that erupted after too many cases of police brutality, the election of Trump and the rise in white supremacy, this question has resurfaced.
- As a consequence, many authors, including **children's books'** authors, have started to show more diversity in stories and history. Multicultural education has been topical and widely researched because it contributes to giving a voice and visibility to minorities. Children from minorities should be able to identify with the protagonists of their stories.

INFO
The Colors of Us, The Skin You Live In, It's Okay to Be Different, Pink Is for Boys are just a few examples of **the new children's literature** that deals with diversity (both ethnic and gender).

II De-whitewashing the past

1 The statue wars

- Columbus Day (traditionally celebrated on the second Monday of October) commemorates Christopher Columbus's arrival in the US. However, since the 1980s, many states on the West coast have started a movement to rename the day Indigenous People's Day to celebrate the indigenous tribes massacred.
- The statue wars around the world emerged around 2015. In the UK, the US and Australia, minorities led symbolic actions against monuments that were seen as white supremacy celebration. Some statues were vandalised, others unsealed as a protest sign.

2 At peace with the past

- In 2021, Canada had to face again the cruel history of boarding schools where indigenous children were whitewashed, stripped off of their cultural heritage. Canada and Australia have engaged in a process of apologies and recognition of that dark history. In the USA, the BLM movement urged people to see how offensive statues of confederate generals are.
- How do we narrate history with an unbiased, neutral perspective? These movements have led to a re-thinking on how we tell history. The purpose is not to erase some historical figures or events, but to build a narrative that englobes all experiences without omitting the sufferings of minorities.

zoOm

Debunking history

- Charlottesville, VA is central to this statue war as it was home to a deadly confrontation between Alt right supporters (white supremacists) and people in favour of removing General Lee's statue in August 2017.
- The African-Americans petitioned to have statues removed, claiming that it is a celebration of pro-slavery generals.

→ Learn more about the removing of statues in Charlotesville : bit.ly/PbacAMC1re_5b

Robert E. Lee statue removed from Charlottesville, VA.

19 The British monarchy: between facts and fiction

En bref *The British monarchy has been at the core of world history for centuries. Fiction has met worldwide success, portraying a double-sided vision of this long-established institution, between praising and denouncing. To what extent does fiction confirm or refute the image the British monarchy wants to convey?*

I Praising monarchy

1 A powerful monarch

■ The Magna Carta, signed by King John in 1215, limited the monarch's prerogatives. Since then, the sovereign has been the **Head of State**, holding constitutional and representational duties → FICHE 9. Thus, the monarch stands more as a symbol of national identity, pride and the cement of the Commonwealth.

■ The Orb handed out to the royal monarch during coronation is the **symbol of godly power**, giving the Queen or King a mesmerising aura. Castles, balls and uniforms match this vision of **superiority**, much in keeping with British greatness, established during **Queen Victoria**'s reign (1837-1901): industrial expansion, economic progress and Empire.

> **INFO**
> **Queen Victoria** reigned over an Empire on which the Sun never set. This was the Victorian age and her people were the Victorians. Victoria Falls (Africa) or the state of Victoria (Australia) are named after her.

2 Monarchs and their peoples

■ This royal grandeur entered people's homes when **Queen Elizabeth's coronation ceremony** was broadcast live on BBC television to millions of people worldwide in 1953. Since then royal magic has been depicted in many films and series.

■ Since 2016 Netflix British American historical drama ***The Crown*** has been portraying Queen Elizabeth II. From Commonwealth world tours to garden parties at Buckingham Palace, to the Queen's official birthday Trooping the Colour, British monarchy often appears in this drama as a rock Her Majesty's subjects cling to.

II Deconstructing clichés

1 Behind the scenes

■ The clean image the UK has been spreading for centuries has also often been **undermined by fiction**. The British Empire which was once British pride and strength is now considered as a **prejudice** considering the oppressive history of colonialism, based on land conquests, exploitation, violence and slavery. 1982 epic historical drama *Gandhi* highlights the life of India's non-violent independence struggle against the UK.

- *Victoria & Abdul* (2017) celebrates 19th century monarchy while denouncing the lack of tolerance the court had towards the Queen's friendship for her Indian spiritual guide and her burka-clad wife.

2 Facing one's destiny

- Every powerful monarch can be touched by fear, loneliness or incertitude. *The King's Speech* (2010) tenderly depicts King George VI's weakness shown to the public when he has to cope with a stammer getting ready to deliver his first war-time radio broadcast. *The Queen* (2006) denounces royal coldness after Diana's death but also shows how lonely a sovereign can be in her decision-making.

- **Princess Diana's death** shows how dramatic public exposure can be. In 2020 Prince Harry and his wife Meghan Markle shocked the world when stepping down from royal duties, announcing this Megxit in a statement on Instagram before an interview with American talk-show host Oprah Winfrey. Is British monarchy still a way of life or is the end looming when even royals leave the boat?

INFO
Lady Diana was Prince Charles's first wife. She died in 1997 in Paris, aged 36, after her car crashed in a tunnel, her driver trying to escape paparazzi. The death of the "People's Princess" caused an unprecedented public grief and her funeral was watched by 2.5 billion people.

zoOm

Queen Elizabeth II, the longest-serving monarch

- 25-year-old Elizabeth II was crowned at Westminster Abbey on June, 2 1953 as Head of the Commonwealth, Queen of the United Kingdom, Canada, Australia, New Zealand, South Africa, Pakistan and Ceylon.

- Elizabeth II wasn't supposed to reign and became Queen because her uncle, King Edward VIII, abdicated. In 1970 she was the first British monarch to buck against royal tradition when she walked to greet crowds of people in person, rather than wave to them from a protected distance. This lead to a true and faithful relationship between the Queen and her people, only questioned during terrible events like Diana's death.

→ Take a walkabout with the Royal family: bit.ly/PbacAMC1re_5c

20 Iconic cities

En bref *The English-speaking world is often symbolised by New York and London. Yet, some cities have also gained the status of iconic cities. Sydney, Lagos or Mumbai are just as prominent, giving a more modern and trendy vision of what they used to be. To what extent can iconic cities define and reshape the English-speaking world?*

I Cities as symbols

1 Iconic landmarks

- Each country has its own symbol. While the Statue of Liberty in New York Harbor stands for the American Dream and the USA's immigration past, Times Square symbolises the hustle and bustle of the city.
- Many landmarks represent England: from Big Ben and the Tower of London to Buckingham Palace and Picadilly Circus, London is the British city par excellence, matching its royal past to its frenzy of activity.
- The Taj Mahal illustrates India's strong historical heritage.

2 Symbols: from evolution to competition

- Varied symbols redefine the vision people have of the English-speaking world. Even if **Uluru** matches Australia's celebration of its Aboriginal roots, Sydney Opera House remains a key symbol of the country.

INFO
Uluru, also known as Ayers Rock, is a large isolated desert rock situated in the Northern Territory of Australia. Sacred to the Aborigines, it is one of Australia's symbols.

- New York skyline has always featured the land of opportunity America recalls. It has taken a new form since 9/11 and the destruction of the Twin Towers: the One World Trade Center has changed the identity of the whole country.

II Reshaping iconic cities

1 Economic revival

- Mumbai is spearheading the position of India as an emerging economic superpower. This megapolis has been spreading across the bay into a New Mumbai, welcoming the 100,000 inhabitants settling every year.
- Dubbed the "Manhattan of Africa", Lagos has become a bustling metropolis, transforming Nigeria and the vision people have of Africa. Modern engineering and technology have made Lagos Eko Atlantic a new self-sufficient and

sustainable city reclaimed from the sea, featuring state-of-the-art urban design, clean water, advanced telecommunication and tree-lines spacious streets.

2 Cities reshaping Black culture milestones

■ When African American people went North during the **Great Migration**, Harlem, one of NYC's neighbourhoods, soon became a bustling place, giving birth to the Harlem Renaissance, an intellectual and cultural movement spanning the 1920s and 1930s. New York City's energy and dynamism has never decreased since.

INFO

During the **Great Migration**, more than 6 million African Americans fled the rural South to settle in cities of the North, Midwest and West of the USA (from the 1920s to 1970).

■ 400 years after the first slave was brought to the USA, Africa is drawing from its roots to turn its main cities into burgeoning creative scenes. Afrochella (Ghana's music, art and culture festival) is the new Coachella (California's giant trendy music festival).

■ African festival matches Afrofuturism, a movement rooted in progress, combining African culture and identity with design, architecture, fashion, technology and science-fiction. From monuments to buildings or installations afrofuturist architects redefine the urban landscape throughout the continent.

zoOm

Architecture in *Black Panther*

■ When released in 2018 Marvel superhero film *Black Panther* immediately became a hit and Black people felt a sense of pride, regarding the film as a cultural moment in Black history.

■ Set in fictional Wakanda, the film depicts a futuristic and alternative uncolonised Africa where architecture embraces cultural heritage and afrofuturist aesthetics. This is exactly what the new African cities are aiming at, through Afrofuturism.

→ Watch this video about the design in Wakanda: bit.ly/PbacAMC1re_5d

MÉMO VISUEL

REPRESENTING
REPRESENTING

Portraying oneself: a distorting image?

Portraying a positive image

- Blockbusters
- American and patriotic **values**
- **Bollywood**, **Irish folklore**...

Self-deprecation

- Political satires and **criticism**
- **Post-colonial**
- Deeply-rooted **racism**

Facing History

Confronting different viewpoints

- **National narrative** = from the dominant white male perspective
- **Collective memory** vs. **History**: taking into account sufferings and dark experiences of minorities
- Contentions

De-whitewashing the past

- Commemorate
- **Statue wars**: vandalisation, unsealing of statues
- Process of **apologies** and recognition

THE WORLD, ONESELF

Portraying the British monarchy

Praising monarchy

- **Magna Carta**, constitutional and representational duties
- Sovereign as Head of State, symbol of **national identity**
- **Royal aura**: coronation, palaces...
- Coming **closer to the people**

Deconstructing clichés

- **Fiction** changing people's vision of monarchy: colonialism, Diana's death
- **Weight of the Crown**: hard to be a monarch

Redefining iconic cities

Cities as symbols

- **Landmarks**: New York and London
- **Taj Mahal**: India's cultural heritage from the Commonwealth
- Towards **new symbols**: NYC's One World Trade Center since 9/11

Reshaping emblematic cities

- Cities as key elements of evolution: **Harlem Renaissance** (USA), **Afrofuturism** (Africa)
- **Emerging cities**: Mumbai (India), Lagos (Nigeria)

SE TESTER QUIZ

Vérifiez que vous avez bien compris les points clés des **fiches 17 à 20**.

1 Self-portrait: a distorting mirror?

→ FICHE 17

Cochez la ou les propositions qui conviennent.

What is post-colonial literature denouncing?

☐ a. deeply-rooted racism ☐ b. white supremacy ☐ c. patriotic values

2 National discourse, identity and communities

→ FICHE 18

1. Cochez la ou les propositions qui conviennent.

Why is the official history contested these days?

☐ a. it erases sufferings of minorities
☐ b. it lacks diversity ☐ c. it is too objective

2. Vrai ou faux ? Cochez la case qui convient.

	V	F
a. The statue wars have happened in the UK and the US only.	☐	☐
b. Columbus Day is a bank holiday celebrated all over the US.	☐	☐
c. Some governments have started a process of apologies for their dark history.	☐	☐

3 The British monarchy

→ FICHE 19

Complétez le texte ci-dessous avec les mots qui conviennent.

In the UK, the monarch doesn't govern the country. He / She has .... and .... duties. Thus, Queen .... rather stands as a .... of national identity. She has had the .... reign so far, since her coronation in .... She is Head of the .... and Queen of the ....

4 Iconic cities

→ FICHE 20

1. Reliez les éléments comme il convient.

a. New York City •	• Picadilly Circus
b. Lagos •	• the One World Trade Center
c. London •	• Eko Atlantic

2. Vrai ou faux ? Cochez la case qui convient.

	V	F
a. In the 19th century, many African Americans left busy US northern cities to move to the rural South.	☐	☐
b. Coachella is a famous cultural festival in Ghana (Africa).	☐	☐
c. Afrofuturism combines African cultural roots with cutting-edge design, fashion, technology and science-fiction.	☐	☐

S'ENTRAÎNER

5 Réviser le cours en 8 questions flash

→ FICHES 17 à 20

1. Why is Hollywood an asset to promote American values worldwide?
2. How does the British film industry portray its society?
3. How can children's books give a voice to minorities?
4. How do some minorities contest official history?
5. Why was Queen Victoria's reign so meaningful and prestigious?
6. What images of the British monarchy do fictions convey?
7. Which iconic city represents the English-speaking world the best? Why?
8. Why is Lagos called the "Manhattan of Africa"?

6 Analyser une image

→ FICHE 18

Observez l'image et répondez aux questions.

Document A

Monument to the Women of World War II,
John W. Mills, London, 2005.

INFO
As thousands of men were away serving in the army during WW2, **British women were conscripted in 1941**, given the choice to work in factories or in one of the auxiliary services. By 1943, 9 out of 10 single women aged between 20 and 30 had been conscripted. Many women also played a crucial role, running households on the home front.

1. Who does the memorial celebrate? Why?
2. How did the sculptor convey the message? Describe the memorial and explain what it symbolises.
3. This memorial was inaugurated in July 2005 by Queen Elizabeth II. How meaningful is it?

7 Comprendre un article de presse

→ FICHE 18

Lisez le texte et répondez aux questions.

Document B 'It's a beautiful day for democracy': Virginia removes Robert E. Lee statue from capital

The article from The Guardian *is explaining the symbol behind the removal of Robert E. Lee's statue in Richmond, VA.*

Elated crowd cheered the removal of the bronze monument to Confederate general, erected more than 130 years ago in Richmond.

For 131 years it loomed over Richmond, Virginia, once the capital of America's slave-owning south, sending a chilling message about the resi lience of white supremacy to generations that passed beneath.

But at 8.55 am on Wednesday, daylight reappeared between a giant statue of the Confederate general Robert E. Lee and its granite pedestal, now covered with Black Lives Matter graffiti. In warm sunshine the towering sculpture was hoisted[1] by work crews and lowered to the ground amid cheers, songs and whoops from a watching crowd.

No one believed that the final humbling of insurrectionist Lee or the removal of a bronze monument, albeit[2] one of the biggest to the Confederacy, was going to fix systemic racism overnight. But in the moment there was elation[3] after a decades-long campaign galvanised by last year's racial justice pro tests that followed the police killing of George Floyd in faraway Minneapolis.

"It's a beautiful day for democracy," said a 47-year-old man who gave his name as Rig and carried a monochrome version of the Stars and Stripes that bore the words "Black Lives Matter" and a raised fist.

"It's time for us to be honest about our history. Germany has zero statues of Hitler or Rommel. They learned the lesson and we have to learn the lesson: we cannot coddle[4] white supremacy in this country."

Lee was the most prominent southern general in the 1861-65 civil war that ended in victory for the Union led by President Abraham Lincoln. But decades after the conflict hundreds of Confederate statues were erected in a sweeping reassertion of white power, often in the cities with the biggest African American populations. [...]

For more than a century the statue was a constant reminder to Richmond's Black residents of generational slavery. Four years ago Mitch Landrieu, then the mayor of New Orleans, where another Lee statue was removed in 2017, wondered what it would be like for African American parents to explain to their daughter why Lee stood atop their city. "Can you look into that young girl's eyes and convince her that Robert E. Lee is there to encourage her?" he asked. "Do you think she will feel inspired and hopeful by that story?"

Civil rights activists had long called for the Lee statue in Richmond to be removed only to run into a brick wall with city and state officials. But after Floyd's death sparked[5] a nationwide uprising during the presidency of Donald Trump, the area around the statue became a hub for protests and occasional clashes with police.

Lee's pedestal has been covered by constantly evolving, colorful graffiti, with many of the painted messages denouncing police and demanding an end to systemic racism and inequality. [...]

David Smith, *The Guardian*, September 8, 2021,

1. hoist: lift
2. albeit: although
3. elation: intense joy
4. coddle: indulge
5. spark: lead to

1. Who was **General Lee**? Explain why his statue had become an issue.

INFO
The US Civil War (1861-1865) opposed Abraham Lincoln representing the USA and 11 South Confederate states which had left the Union. Confederate General **Robert Lee** fought against racial equality for African Americans, defending slavery. He soon became a national icon and has remained a symbol of white supremacy.

2. What is celebrated in this article? How did people react to it? Why?

3. How can removing a statue be considered as "rewriting history"?

8 Traduction en français

Répondez aux questions préparatoires, puis traduisez l'article du *Guardian* de « No one believed... » à « and a raised fist » (document B, l. 11-18).

1. Certains groupes nominaux peuvent être complexes. Quel est le mot le plus important, celui qui devra être traduit en premier, dans *"last year's racial justice protests"* (l. 14) ?

2. Le paragraphe commençant par *"No one believed..."* est composé d'une phrase de plus de trois lignes. Doit-on traduire les propositions relatives et les coordinations mot à mot ou doit-on scinder cette longue phrase ?

OBJECTIF BAC

9 Synthèse de documents • History in the (re)making

3 h

Les deux documents A (p. 107) et B (p. 108) que vous venez d'étudier et le document qui va suivre (C) constituent le dossier à analyser pour l'épreuve de synthèse portant sur la thématique « Représentation » et plus particulièrement l'axe « Représenter le monde, se représenter ».

LE SUJET

Prenez connaissance du dossier proposé, composé des documents A, B et C non hiérarchisés, et traitez en anglais le sujet suivant (500 mots maximum) :

Taking into account their specificities, show how the documents illustrate the need for a country to (re)write its history. Make sure to address:
- the difficulty of merging history and duty of remembrance;
- the different possible ways of remembering.

Document C Whose history: the role of statues and monuments in Australia

Taken from the website of an Australian museum, this text weighs the impact of statues commemorating European explorers and their removal.

The removal of statues of racists, such as Cecil Rhodes, or statues that celebrate racist history, such as colonial invasion and slavery in the United States, England and Africa has created discussions in Australia around what should be done [with] its statues and monuments of invaders and colonists, who to many First Nations people are symbols of colonisation and genocide. Many commentators argue against the removal of such statues, saying that they are part of history and stating that their removal would be silencing, erasing and/or rewriting history. However, others would argue that these statues and monuments themselves are rewriting history as they portray men [...] overlooking [their] involvement in the massacres, land theft and oppression of First Nations people.

Why is this an issue? Because these statues and monuments were created to celebrate particular colonisers and colonial events they often do not tell the full story of history and in many cases, they tell a lie. [...] For instance, the statue of James Cook at Hyde Park in Sydney has inscribed at the bottom of it that Cook "discovered this territory 1770" which supports the idea before 1770, Australia was uninhabited, empty land to be discovered which erases the fact that First Nations people have been in Australia for 65,000+ years. By erasing this history, it invalidates First Nations people's rights and claims to their lands.

[...] Writer Tyler Stiem argues that because these statues are usually in public places where people would walk past and see them regularly, it makes them normal, which in turn can make their actions, including violent actions seem normal or something to celebrate. This can make injustices these statues represent easier to defend and again make injustices of today harder to see. [...]

Because of this, many have asked for the removal of statues of people and events involved in First Nations oppression, others have suggested that get reinscribed with a more critical, factual history written on them, while others have said let them stand but build counter monuments to provide a fuller understanding of history. [...]

Nathan mudyi Sentence, www.australian.museum, September 2021,
© Nathan Sentence and the Australian Museum.

▶▶▶ LA FEUILLE DE ROUTE

→ *Reportez-vous à la méthode générale de la synthèse de documents, p. 128-129.*

Étape 1 Analyser les termes du sujet

- *(Re)write :* l'écriture est toujours subjective et rend compte d'une perspective, d'un point de vue. Le « (re) » sous-entend que l'on peut revisiter cette histoire et la rectifier. Cette mémoire collective peut être complétée, nuancée, anesthésiée ou lacunaire.

- *Merging history and duty of remembrance :* la prise en compte de l'histoire, dans toutes ses dimensions, s'inscrit dans un devoir de souvenir, de commémoration du passé.

- *Ways of remembering :* les moyens pour commémorer cette mémoire collective sont les musées, les reconstitutions, les statues, les monuments, mais aussi les livres d'histoire, la tradition orale...

Étape 2 Lire et analyser le corpus à la lumière de la problématique

- Problématiques : In a context of minorities trying to have their voice heard, how is history a tool to assert one's rights and place in society?

Are statues and monuments' removal a step towards an inclusive society?

Étape 3 Analyser et comparer l'apport de chaque document

	Remembering the past	Overlooked elements	A positive step
Doc. A Monument	reaffirming the role of women in WW2		inauguration by the Queen = official recognition
Doc. B Article		questioning the balance of power in society: more important to celebrate a racist past or to not pursue racial divide?	New Orleans in 2017: created a movement, a trend in removing statues
Doc. C Article	• colonialism, slavery, segregation, discrimination • telling lies • silencing, erasing part of history	• example of the statue in Hyde Park Sydney • negation of the existence of Aboriginals before the arrival of James Cook	• today's injustices recognised • in public place no need for monuments to remember the past (see example of Germany) • different solutions to tackle the issue: counter monuments, clear inscriptions on the monuments, removal of monuments

Étape 4 Construire le plan de la synthèse

I. Facing a dark past?

II. History overlooked

III. "It's a beautiful day for democracy"

Étape 5 Rédiger la synthèse → CORRIGÉ p. 115

CORRIGÉS

SE TESTER QUIZ

1 Self-portrait: a distorting mirror?

Réponses a et b. Post-colonial literature denounces deeply-rooted racism and white supremacy.

2 National discourse, identity and communities

1. Réponses a et b. Official history is contested because it erases sufferings of minorities and lacks diversity.
2. a. Faux. Statue wars happened all over the world, including Australia and South Africa as well.
b. Faux. It has been contested, especially on the West coast.
c. Vrai. Canada for instance apologised many times over the past 30 years for their part in undermining First Nations.

3 The British monarchy

In the UK, the Monarch doesn't govern the country. He / She has constitutional and representational duties. Thus, Queen Elizabeth II rather stands as a symbol of national identity. She has had the longest reign so far, since her coronation in 1953. She is Head of the Commonwealth and Queen of the UK.

4 Iconic cities

1. a. New York City: the One World Trade Center • b. Lagos: Eko Atlantic • c. London: Picadilly Circus
2. a. Faux. In the 20th century more than 6 million African Americans left the rural South and the segregation laws to start a new life in northern cities.
b. Faux. Coachella is a famous cultural festival in California, USA. Afrochella takes place in Ghana (Africa).
c. Vrai. Afrofuturism combines African cultural roots with cutting-edge design, fashion, technology and science-fiction. It is a way for Africa to rewrite its own story.

INFO
The film *Black Panther* displays what **Afrofuturism** is (fashion, architecture, technology…).

S'ENTRAÎNER

5 Réviser le cours en 8 questions flash

1. Hollywood is a big part of the promotion of American values abroad. The movie industry is powerful internationally and the positive image displayed contributes to showing American strengths and powers.
2. The British film industry tends to point out British flaws. Their satirical tone conveys a political and social comment on what is wrong in British society.

3. Children's books' authors have been increasingly aware of the need to show diversity in their characters in order to be more visible and so that children will identify with good role models that look like them.
4. Minorities have used many means to have their voice heard and their visibility recognised: from renaming bank holidays, to more violent actions of vandalism of statues and monuments.
5. Queen Victoria's reign (1837-1901) turned Britain into a worldwide empire on which the sun never set. The Victorian era was marked by industrial and scientific changes mostly triggered by the industrial revolution.
6. Fiction portrays the British monarchy as an untouchable class, depicting ceremonies, palaces, balls and royal world tours. But we are also shown how lonely and criticised a monarch can be.
7. New York and London tend to be replaced by new iconic cities such as the bustling cities of Lagos (Nigeria) and Mumbai (India) which take the lead and write a new chapter in the vision people have of the English-speaking world.
8. The Nigerian mega-city of Lagos is turning into a financial hub. Eko Atlantic is a project of urban development meant to welcome 250,000 inhabitants and 150,000 workers with skyscrapers, efficient transport, offices and shops.

6 Analyser une image

1. This memorial celebrates women who played a crucial role in WW2. Men who fought on the battlefields are often commemorated but women tend to be forgotten. This memorial recalls their war effort.
2. This memorial represents a high and large bronze panel. Many different uniforms and working clothes worn by women during WW2 are represented on each side of the memorial. The sculptor conveys the idea that these clothes were hung after the war, when women went back to their everyday lives, as they would have done at the end of a day's work. The memorial celebrates these women's massive war effort, which is often overlooked.
3. Queen Elizabeth II always supported British people during WW2, be they soldiers, workers or civilians. This royal recognition makes this memorial all the more official and formal. Being a woman, the Queen insists on the value given to women in general.

INFO
During WW2, **Princess Elisabeth**, aged 19, joined the Auxiliary Territorial Service (ATS) where she trained as a driver and mechanic.

7 Comprendre un article de presse

1. Robert Lee was a Confederate general who led some Southern states which had decided to leave the US union into the 1861-1865 Civil War. Even if the Confederates lost the war, Lee has remained one of the symbols of white supremacy, in favour of slavery. His statue in Richmond and many others are shocking landmarks of US history.
2. 131 years after it was erected in Richmond, Virginia, one of Lee's most famous statues was removed officially. Covered with Black Lives Matter graffiti for months,

this statue had taken a new symbolism, representing the fight against racism. People were overjoyed, cheering, singing and whooping.
3. If a statue symbolises some key historical landmarks or famous people who played an important role in history, removing it means reorienting the message a country sends to the coming generations. In this case, praising Lee and white supremacy was conspicuous and that vision offended African Americans. Condemning the statue means the USA doesn't agree with white supremacy anymore.

8 Traduction en français

1. Dans un groupe nominal, le terme le plus important est placé à la fin. Les éléments qui le précèdent viennent le déterminer, le spécifier. Il faut donc commencer par traduire le dernier terme puis dérouler la traduction de droite à gauche.
2. Il faut parfois couper des phrases longues afin de rester compréhensible.
Voici la traduction proposée.
Personne n'a cru que la dernière leçon d'humilité donnée à l'insurgé Lee ou que le retrait d'un monument en bronze, bien qu'il ait été un des plus grands de la Confédération, allait supprimer le racisme systémique du jour au lendemain. Mais sur le moment il y a eu de l'euphorie. La campagne, commencée il y a des décennies, a été galvanisée l'an dernier par les protestations prônant la justice raciale, suite à la mort de George Floyd tué par un policier dans le lointain Minneapolis.
« C'est un beau jour pour la démocratie, » dit Rig, un homme de 47 ans qui portait une version monochrome de la bannière étoilée représentant un poing levé avec l'inscription « Black Lives Matter ».

OBJECTIF BAC

9 Synthèse de documents • History in the (re)making

Les titres en couleur et les puces permettent de mettre en évidence la structure du corrigé mais ils ne figureraient pas sur une copie de bac.

Introduction

Statues have been at the center of a new debate regarding the offense minorities feel towards the dominant white perspective they display. Countries face a difficult introspection, trying to find a balance between a duty of remembrance and an inclusive vision of past events. So how is history a tool to assert one's rights and place in society?

Facing a dark past?

- Monuments, statues, **bank holidays** are intended to celebrate the past. They work as a commemoration of historical events or figures.

> **INFO**
> **Columbus Day**, celebrated on the second Monday of October, was officially recognised by President Biden as Indigenous People's Day in 2021.

- As stated in the blurb from the museum (C), some people think that the "removal would be silencing, erasing and/or rewriting history". The three verbs "silencing", "erasing" "rewriting" are at the core of our question. The visibility of such monuments in public places (C) aims at facing past events, even if they are painful.

■ Document A functions as a counter argument to this "silencing" as the statue repairs a forgotten aspect of World War 2. By promoting the role of women in World War 2, the commemorative statue gives voice to a minority that was overlooked.

History overlooked

■ From a different perspective, some people argue that these statues and monuments are themselves proof of a white-dominant view on history, negating the existence or exploits of minorities (B and C).

■ The examples given in both documents B and C highlight how the writing of history is subjective. Whitewashing starts with the promotion of European explorers or white generals.

■ The psychological impact of these monuments and statues is discussed in both texts, stating that as a member of a minority, seeing the celebration and commemoration of people who massacred your ancestors is proof of systemic racism.

It's a beautiful day for democracy

■ The removal of statues of Confederate generals in the south of the US (B) or the official inauguration of World War 2 memorial by the Queen (A) are both equally important for a more inclusive democracy. It shows past injustices are in the process of being repaired.

■ Despite a – at times – violent movement to get rid of any signs of racism (B and C), this surge of civil actions are a positive sign that society is ready to face its past and the present consequences.

■ If there are no statues or monuments of Hitler in Germany (C), it hasn't prevented the country from learning from its past and moving forward. Black Lives Matter toys with the same idea that celebrating racism, segregation and slavery through monuments and statues is no way for a society to face its racial divide. Instead, it should acknowledge its past to better deal with a growing white supremacist group.

Conclusion

As a celebratory monument, statues remind us of a past that can be offensive to minorities and our modern society needs to face its whitewashed perspective on history and repair the offense they display towards minorities around the Commonwealth.

(508 words)

6 Faire une synthèse de documents

Réussir la synthèse suppose de maîtriser les caractéristiques de tous types de documents et d'en rendre compte de façon objective, concise et ordonnée.

21 Analysing fiction

En bref *It is first necessary to consider the text globally: find out what is said and who about. Then you have to concentrate on the writer's choices so as to access to full understanding.*

I Global understanding

1 The characters and the setting

- When reading the extract for the first time, it is necessary to find out **basic facts** such as who does what and where and when it takes place. It is useful to pick up various clues.

Elements of the text	Interpretation
Pronouns and possessive determiners	Identify the character·s clearly
Adjectives	Analyse the characters' appearances and personalities as well as elements related to the setting
References to time and space	Determine the historical and geographical background

- Chronological and logical link words give clues as to the **chain of events and key moments of the plot**. It is thus useful to find out if the events are told according to the chronological order or if there are flashbacks or flashforwards.

2 The narrator and point of view

- It is necessary to identify the narrator who tells the story and from whose point of view the story is told so as to **fully understand the narrative**.

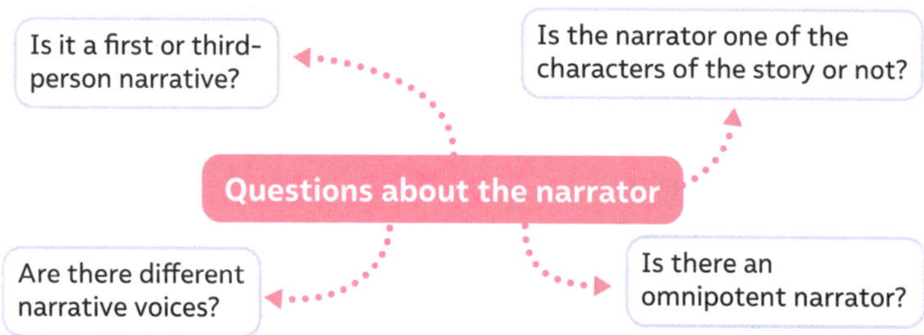

- The **narrator's role and stance** do affect what the narrative tells and the way it is told. For example with an omnipotent narrator, the reader knows more than the characters, whereas with an objective narrator, the reader knows as much as the characters.

II Detailed understanding

1 Language

- The use of language (whether formal, colloquial or use of slang), the tone (whether ironical, humorous or tragic...), the atmosphere (whether stressful, conflicting or quiet...) of the extract are equally important and help to understand the main theme·s.

- Figures of speech play the same role. Whether they stress similarity, repetition or contrast, they always contribute to spotting the key ideas, themes or features.

  Frankenstein ***or the modern Prometheus***, by Mary Shelley

  (This full version of the title comprises an allusion to the ancient myth of Prometheus.)

- Focusing on how long the sentences are or the tenses used, leads to an in-depth understanding of the extract. For example, short sentences may be used to account for a character's stream of consciousness.

  Was it possible they heard not? Almighty God! – no, no! They heard! – they suspected! – they knew! – they were making a mockery of my horror! – this I thought, and this I think. *The Tell-Tale Heart*, by E. A. Poe

2 Unknown vocabulary

- You should not panic when there are words you do not understand. Use different strategies so as to deduce what they mean. First observe the word in context: look at the preceding and following words, consider the nature of the word (noun, adjective, adverb, verb...). It gives useful clues to guess its meaning.

- You can then consider word formation processes. → FICHE 31

zoom

What to look for when annotating?

Here are some ideas. Use different colours to underline the text.

Structure	• simple or multi-clause sentences • paragraph: how it opens or closes • repeated words and phrases • order of ideas in the excerpt
Language	• use of formal or standard English, colloquialism or slang • literary devices • words with particular connotation
Characterisation and voice	• key elements showing the development of characters • clues about the main voice • story told in first or third-person
Themes and ideas	any words or phrases that link to the main themes or a particular semantic field

22 Analysing non-fiction

En bref *Non-fiction can be divided into several types of texts which all aim at influencing, convincing, persuading or defending a point of view. When dealing with such a text, it is necessary to identify what sort of text it is, to analyse its structure and the linguistic devices used so as to understand the arguments which are developed.*

I Identifying the type of text

1 Press articles

- The sources, title and subtitles clearly point to press articles. Yet, there are different sorts of articles: leading articles (*articles de fond*), columns (*chroniques*), editorials (*éditoriaux*) or reviews (*critiques*).
- Even if they have a different structure, editorials, columns and reviews are subjective and express the opinion of the newspaper, the journalist or critic.

2 Critical texts, essays and speeches

- Essays, speeches and book or film reviews put arguments forward in using a clear structure: arguments and examples are carefully and gradually organised so as to back up a particular thesis.
- Formal language is used: long, often complex, sentences and specific vocabulary or imagery. Being able to pick up **simple sentences** helps to understand the text.

> **INFO**
> A **simple sentence** is composed of the elements that are absolutely necessary to grab its meaning: subject, verb, complement.

II Identifying the structure

1 Argumentation

- The main sequence in an argumentative text is composed of:
  - an introduction: it presents the theme or issue and what is at stake;
  - a body with arguments: it presents and defends the thesis (arguments, examples, references, testimonies, quotations, comparisons, anecdotes, precisions, refutation, counter-arguments);
  - a conclusion: it rephrases the thesis, sums up the justification and gives the final position.
- The first sentence of each paragraph always gives key information which is then further developed.

  Most people have no idea how advanced the technology has become: now faces can be tracked from half a mile away thanks to software called Intelligence Pedestrian Surveillance.

2 | Arguments and examples

The writer proves his·her thesis thanks to arguments: the substantive reasons that justify it to convince the readers. Arguments have a general scope while examples deal with particular instances and illustrate arguments; they prove how relevant arguments are with a real case.

> It takes a lot of courage to whistleblowers to reveal sensitive information. (general scope) After revealing international spying by the NSA, Edward Snowden fled to Hong Kong then to Moscow in order not to be jailed. (particular instance)

III Being familiar with characteristics

1 | Link words

Link words (conversely, obviously, besides...) are used to relate these arguments and examples. They establish logical connections between the ideas that are developed: cause, consequence, explanation, illustration, listing, comparison, contrast, compromising, conclusion... That's why it is necessary to pick them out.

2 | Figures of speech and abstract vocabulary

- Figures of speech are used to give a forceful demonstration whether to argue for or against a thesis. Repetitions hammer it home. Comparisons assert similarities in a positive or negative way. Hyperbole uses exaggeration for effect:

  > Millions of school children every year... (in a speech against school uniforms)

- There are many abstract words linked to ideas, notions, feelings and emotions.

zoOm

How to detect the author's opinion

Various devices can be used to give one's opinion.

Persuasive devices

- Derogatory suffixes, modal / specific adverbs and vocabulary to make a positive or negative comment.
- Modals and perception verbs to express will or necessity, certainty or doubt.
- 3rd person pronouns to point to unbiased statements.
- 1st person pronouns to claim commitment.

23 Analysing a picture

En bref *Pictures are meant to be looked at, to attract people's attention and to strike their imagination or to give a message. Their aim may be information, protest, ideology or personal representation. They require a specific language that needs deciphering so as to understand the artist's message. In order to decipher a picture, various steps are necessary.*

I Identifying and describing

1 Nature and origin

First identify the nature of the picture: it can be a photograph, a caricature, a cartoon, a street art painting, a propaganda poster, etc. Pick up all relevant information you can find: title, artist's name, date. If the picture is coupled with a **caption**, read it carefully, as it will help you define the main topic of the picture and its social and historical context.

> **INFO**
> **Caption:** title or brief explanation or comment accompanying an illustration.

2 Structure and content

- You can then pay attention to the layout (*disposition*), then the setting and characters of your document.
- The layout is very important as it gives clues: the number of parts, the positioning (find out the focal point), the colours, light and shading, contrasts, the arrangements of volumes and shapes are key features that help understand the overall effect.
- Before describing what takes place, it is necessary to locate the scene so as to avoid misinterpreting the picture under study. When describing the characters always examine carefully their gestures, actions, body language, gaze and facial expressions.
- All these elements provide the general atmosphere conveyed by the picture.

II Construing and interpreting the intentions

1 Personal impressions and symbols

- To analyse the artist's intentions, first concentrate on the emotions the picture arouses when you look at it. Try to describe what the image spontaneously evokes in you both positively and negatively, and what it is in the picture that makes you feel that way.

- Secondly identify the **symbolic** elements the picture contains. For example you can wonder if the doves represented in your picture stand for peace or if the colour red means danger, love or prohibition.

INFO

A **symbol** is a thing that stands for something else. Usually, it consists of a real object used to represent something more abstract or complex.

2 The artist's goals

- To fully understand the artist's message, focus on the cultural, historical or artistic context as it may give further significant information. Relate them to all your findings so as to stress the artist's intentions.
- You should consider the purpose for which the image was created. Attempts to influence? To sell something? To denounce a situation? Who is the picture aimed at?

zoOm

How to situate the various elements in a picture

So as to describe what you can see as precisely as possible, use these prepositions.

24 Analysing a chart or a map

En bref *All graphs or maps tell a story. They use figures, dates or colours to help viewers understand the meaning and impact of the information presented. You will have to use the graphical elements, context and your personal knowledge to pinpoint the emerging trends.*

I Identifying and describing

1 Types of graphs and maps

■ To describe accurately the distinct elements of visual data, start by identifying the type of map or graph presented. There are various types of graphs: **line graphs** show how something changes over time; **bar charts** compare different aspects; **pie charts** show how an aspect is divided into different parts or sectors.

> **VOCABULARY**
> **line graph**: diagramme en courbe
> **bar chart**: histogramme
> **pie chart**: camembert

■ Similarly, maps can be of different kinds. Physical maps highlight geographical natural features. Political maps focus on borders. Economic maps point to economic activity and natural resources. Population maps show population density in different areas.

2 Gathering information

■ Focus on the date (if relevant), the source (paying a particular attention to its reliability), then the name of the author.

■ In order to determine the content of this document first try to decipher what the title and key (or legend) tell you. Then focus on axes, labels or the colours of the map to gather more information, for example, graduating colour schemes (from darker to lighter shades) highlight a progression from lower to higher values. Then describe the main aspects emphasised by the graph or the map and finally pay attention to any major changes and / or differences.

II Interpreting and concluding

■ You must determine trends and explain the relationship between and among the various items as well as the reasons for the changes and / or differences you have noticed. Considering the background (current events, history...) enables you to shed light on the main points or aspects you get from the chart or map.

■ Thanks to the results of your analysis, you must explain and specify what they tell you about the topic. Try to answer these questions: What are the map or graph showing? What is its aim? Can you notice any form of bias?

III Choosing the right words

1 Dealing with an evolution

going up	an increase (in) • a rise • a growth • a peak (in) to increase (by) • to rise (by) • to grow • to peak • to soar
going down	a fall • a decrease (in) • a drop • a decline (in) to fall • to decrease • to decline • to collapse
going up and down	a fluctuation (in) • a dip (in) to fluctuate • to dip • to vary
remaining stable	to remain stable / steady • to level off • to level out
top	to reach a peak / a climax / its highest level
bottom	to bottom out • to sink to a trough / the lowest level

2 Comparing and explaining

Describing trends, differences, or stages requires the use of comparison structure words and phrases, link words as well as comparatives and superlatives.

- Key words to express **similarity**: similarly, likewise, equally, alike, identical...
  Similarly, the employment opportunities are equally diverse.
- Key words to **contrast**: unlike, in comparison with, contrary to, though, even though, different from, whereas, while, and yet...
  In comparison with Scotland, Wales voted to leave the EU.

zoOm

Deciphering a map or a graph

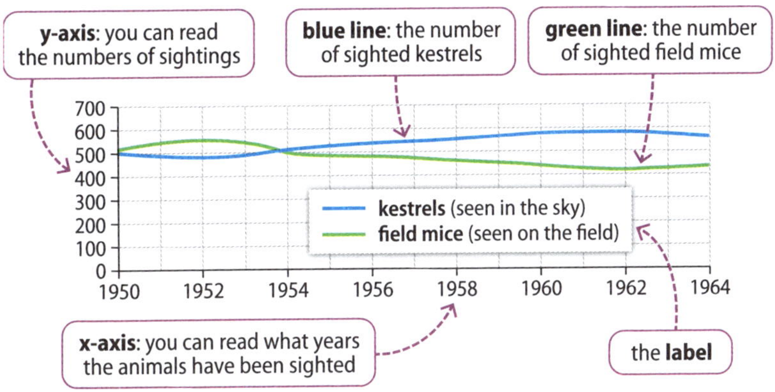

25 La synthèse

En bref *La synthèse vise à mettre en lumière les relations entre les documents proposés et ne consiste pas en une énumération de thèmes communs. Cet exercice nécessite au préalable une analyse détaillée de chacun des documents.*

I Lire le dossier et rechercher les axes communs

1 Découvrir le dossier dans son ensemble

- Il faut d'abord prendre connaissance de la ou des **question·s** accompagnant les documents et en analyser tous les termes clés, afin d'identifier les différents éléments mis en tension qui justifient la question posée.
- Il faut ensuite identifier la nature des supports proposés, les indications périphériques (titres, sources et natures des documents) qui fournissent des éléments indispensables. Le but est ici d'avoir à l'esprit le **thème général du dossier**.

2 Procéder à l'analyse détaillée

- Il est indispensable de considérer chaque document dans sa **spécificité de forme et de contenu** avant de procéder à la synthèse proprement dite.
- Il faut procéder aux **premiers relevés** sur chaque document séparément à l'aide de surligneurs de différentes couleurs :

Relevés à effectuer

- Le **genre** et l'**idée générale**.
- La **manière** dont les éléments sont évoqués (tonalité du document).
- Les **détails pertinents** au regard de la question posée.
- Ce qui relève du **factuel** et de l'**implicite** (ce que l'auteur suggère au-delà des mots en utilisant un champ lexical ou des figures de style).

3 Effectuer l'étude comparative

- Il convient ensuite de procéder à une étude comparative des documents. Les consignes qui guident la synthèse permettent d'élaborer un **tableau synoptique**. Il donne une vue d'ensemble des différents repérages pour chaque document.

CONSEIL

Le **tableau synoptique** comprend autant de colonnes que de documents. On peut y ajouter une colonne supplémentaire intitulée : pistes de réflexion.

- Le tableau doit faire apparaître les similarités ou les différences autour de notions ou de mots clés qui pourront relever aussi bien du contenu thématique (la folie, la ville, la pauvreté…) que de données structurelles (point de vue, mode de représentation…) ou esthétiques (gothique, pop'art…).

II Élaborer le plan et rédiger la synthèse

1 Construire le plan

Les différentes questions ou consignes du sujet correspondent aux différentes parties du plan. Celui-ci doit être clair et apporter une réponse à la question déterminée par l'analyse du sujet.

2 Rédiger la synthèse

- L'introduction doit comporter une amorce, il faut présenter la thématique du dossier, caractériser rapidement chacun des documents, puis reformuler la problématique et annoncer les étapes de la démonstration, c'est-à-dire le plan.
- Le développement doit suivre le plan. Il est constitué de paragraphes dans lesquels il faut avancer des arguments reposant sur les éléments repérés dans l'analyse. Le propos doit être cohérent, les causes et conséquences clairement établies. Chaque argument doit être illustré par un ou des exemple·s et s'appuyer sur les différents documents. Il faut veiller à soigner les transitions.
- Le rôle de la conclusion est de répondre à la question présentée dans l'introduction. Elle dresse un bilan du devoir mais il faut éviter les redites et pour cela, veiller à reformuler les conclusions partielles énoncées à la fin de chaque partie. Attention, la conclusion ne doit jamais contenir d'idées nouvelles.

zoOm

Rédiger un écrit complémentaire

Dans certains sujets, la synthèse demandée ne doit faire que 300 mots, mais vous devez rédiger en plus un écrit de type argumentatif de 200 mots.

Objectifs

- Développer un point de vue nuancé à partir d'une citation d'un des textes du dossier.
- Expliquer en quoi elle éclaire ou non les différents documents du dossier.

Étape 1 : reformulez la citation.

Étape 2 : présentez une idée ou un aspect développé dans le ou les documents qui corrobore la citation ou au contraire s'y oppose.

NB : cet écrit étant court, une conclusion n'est pas nécessaire.

MÉMO VISUEL

RÉUSSIR

1 Analyser le sujet

- Repérez et définissez les **termes clés** du sujet
- Mettez-les en **relation** avec la thématique du dossier
- Formulez une **problématique**

5 Rédiger la synthèse

Rédigez l'introduction

- Commencez par une **amorce**
- Reformulez le **sujet**
- Annoncez le **plan**

Construisez le développement

- Faites **apparaître clairement** les parties et sous-parties
- Mettez en **tension** les différents documents, en les **citant** tous et en dégageant clairement leurs structures et enjeux implicites
- Soignez les **transitions** entre les différents éléments

Rédigez la conclusion

Répondez clairement à votre problématique

LA SYNTHÈSE

2 Lire et analyser le corpus

- Identifiez la **thématique** du dossier et les différents **types de document**
- Relevez les **idées importantes**

3 Analyser et comparer l'apport de chaque document

- Construisez un tableau synoptique pour avoir une **vue de l'ensemble** des documents et de votre analyse
- Complétez le tableau avec des **exemples** précis et référencés

4 Construire le plan

À l'aide de votre analyse du sujet et du tableau synoptique :
- reformulez et **précisez** les pistes données dans le sujet
- dégagez les **grandes parties du plan** qui en découlent
- complétez le **plan détaillé**, avec les sous-parties

SE TESTER QUIZ

Vérifiez que vous avez bien compris les points clés des **fiches 21 à 25**.

1 Analyser un texte

→ FICHES **21** et **22**

1. Identifiez la nature du texte (*speech*, *article*, *novel*).

a. "Elon Musk's company Neuralink released a video showing how its chip implant could allow a monkey to play video games using its brain."
Extract from ....

b. "Today, it is an honour for me to be speaking again after a long time."
Extract from ....

c. "He stood before me, perfectly still in the gloom of the winter's night."
Extract from ....

2. Associez chaque type d'écrit journalistique à ce qu'il exprime.

a. an editorial •	• news
b. news analysis •	
c. a review •	• personal opinion of the writer
d. news article •	

2 Analyser un graphique

→ FICHE **24**

Observez le graphique de la page 125 et indiquez les dates correspondant aux affirmations.

a. The graph shows a low point of the mice line and a high point for the kestrel's line. It's a turning point for both lines: ....

b. The graph depicts a peak of the mice line and a slight drop of the kestrel's line. It's a turning point for both lines: ....

c. The graph outlines an intersection point between the lines: ....

3 Rédiger la synthèse

→ FICHE **25**

Cochez la ou les affirmations correctes.

☐ a. A synoptic chart provides a general overview of the various documents.
☐ b. A synoptic chart enables you to compare the documents easily.
☐ c. You should include a brief characterisation of each document in the introduction.
☐ d. You should give the outline of your demonstration in the introduction.
☐ e. You should give your answer to the question in the introduction.
☐ f. You should give your opinion on the documents in the conclusion.
☐ g. You should make an assessment and answer the question in the conclusion.

S'ENTRAÎNER

Les trois documents (A, p. 131, B, p. 133 et C, p. 134) constituent le dossier à analyser pour l'épreuve de synthèse portant sur la thématique « Représentation » et plus particulièrement l'axe « Faire entendre sa voix ». L'épreuve est ici décomposée en plusieurs exercices préparatoires.

Prenez connaissance du dossier proposé, composé des documents A, B et C non hiérarchisés, et traitez en anglais le sujet suivant (500 mots maximum) :
Taking into account their specificities, show how the documents illustrate the power of civil actions in fighting racial discrimination.

4 Analyser le sujet

1. In a chart, list the different "civil actions" and associate qualities and purpose to each of those "civil actions".

Civil actions	Qualities and purpose
•	• ....
•	• ....
•	• ....
•	• ....

2. What kind of question can you formulate for your assignment?

5 Lire le corpus

Lisez attentivement les documents, puis présentez-les brièvement.

Document A Black Lives Matter May Be the Largest Movement in US History

The recent Black Lives Matter protests peaked on June 6, when half a million people turned out[1] in nearly 550 places across the United States. That was a single day in more than a month of protests that still continue to today. [...] Four recent polls – including one released this week by Civis Analytics, a data science firm that works with businesses and Democratic campaigns – suggest that about 15 million to 26 million people in the United States have participated in demonstrations over the death of George Floyd and others in recent weeks. [...]

These figures would make the recent protests the largest movement in the country's history, according to interviews with scholars and crowd-counting experts.

Protests against racism and police violence per day

"The geographic spread of protest is a really important characteristic and helps signal the depth and breadth of a movement's support," said Kenneth Andrews, a sociology professor. [...]

The protests may also be benefitting from a country that is more conditioned to protesting. The adversarial stance[2] that the Trump administration has taken on issues like guns, climate change and immigration has led to more protests than under any other presidency since the Cold War. [...]

Who is protesting

More than 40 percent of counties in the United States – at least 1,360 – have had a protest. Unlike with past Black Lives Matter protests, nearly 95 percent of counties that had a protest recently are majority white, and nearly three-quarters of the counties are more than 75 percent white. [...]

According to the Civis Analytics poll, the movement appears to have attracted protesters who are younger and wealthier. The age group with the largest share of protesters was people under 35 and the income group with the largest share of protesters was those earning more than $150,000.

Half of those who said they protested said that this was their first time getting involved with a form of activism or demonstration. [...]

The amount of change that the protests have been able to produce in such a short period of time is significant. In Minneapolis, the City Council pledged to dismantle its police department. In New York, lawmakers repealed a law that kept police disciplinary records secret. Cities and states across the country passed new laws banning chokeholds[3]. Mississippi lawmakers voted to retire their state flag, which prominently includes a Confederate battle emblem. [...]

"It looks, for all the world, like these protests are achieving what very few do: setting in motion a period of significant, sustained, and widespread social, political change," Professor McAdam said. "We appear to be experiencing a social change tipping point[4] – that is as rare in society as it is potentially consequential."

Larry Buchanan, Quoctrung Bui and Jugal K. Patel,
The New York Times, July 3, 2020.

1. turn out: participate
2. stance: opinion, attitude
3. chokehold: gripping someone by the neck
4. tipping point: peak, top

Document B Ahmaud Arbery: trial of accused murderers is test for racial justice 'in the heart of white supremacy'

The trial of the three men, who have pleaded not guilty, occurs six months after the conviction of Derek Chauvin, the white former police officer who murdered George Floyd in Minneapolis after pinning his neck to the ground for nine minutes and 29 seconds. That trial was undoubtedly a landmark moment for police reform advocates around the country, but, say many observers, the case of Ahmaud Arbery is a sterner litmus[1] test for the state of racial justice in the US. [...]

The legal particulars of this murder trial also point to history as well. The McMichaels' defense is expected to hinge[2] on a now defunct Georgia law that traces its roots to the state's era of slavery and essentially allowed private citizens the power to arrest people if they had "reasonable and probable grounds of suspicion" of a felony being committed. In the wake of mass protest following Arbery's death, Georgia's Republican governor repealed the law, but attorneys for all three defendants are expected to utilize it throughout the trial. [...]

The past two weeks have also highlighted the difficulties in impaneling[3] a jury in this small rural county, composed of 69% white residents and 26% Black residents, and which voted 61% for Donald Trump in the 2020 presidential election. [...]

For a case that is tied so deeply to atrocities of the past, the murder of Ahmaud Arbery is also closely linked to prosecutions from recent memory. The presence of eyewitness video, filmed by Bryan as he took part in the pursuit from behind, is set to play a pivotal role in the case. It took months for the footage to emerge, as the case sat in relative obscurity away from the gaze of most national media. The absence of publicly available footage undoubtedly contributed to the initial decision not to indict[4] the three men now standing trial. It was not until the video was made public that the case was handed to Georgia state investigators who promptly recommended charges against the accused. [...] In the same way that Darnella Frazier's eyewitness video of the murder of George Floyd thrust the incident into global consciousness and played a pivotal role at the trial of Derek Chauvin, so too does this footage hold the key to the case.

Oliver Laughland, *The Guardian*, November 3, 2021

1. litmus: decisive for judgement
2. hinge: depend on
3. impaneling: selecting
4. indict: charge

INFO

Ahmaud Arbery, 25, was chased by three armed white men who saw him running past their house and assumed he was a burglar. He was then shot by one of the men during a fight. The event took place on February 23, 2020 in Georgia.

Document C

Mural outside the Daryl Roth Theatre (NYC), Steve "ESPO" Powers.

6 Analyser et comparer l'apport de chaque document

1. Listez les arguments de chaque document dans un tableau, en vous aidant des questions proposées.

Doc A Press article	• What are the specificities of the BLM movement? • What has BLM managed to achieve? • According to Pr McAdam, how effective has this movement been?
Doc B Press article	• What is the legal context of this trial? • How important are video footage in trials involving racial discrimination? • Why are legal actions so important?
Doc C Mural	• What are the elements composing this mural? • What is the artist trying to convey? • How powerful is a mural displayed in the streets to raise awareness?

2. Choisissez trois couleurs et surlignez, dans le tableau, les idées qui vous semblent similaires ou opposées afin de faire ressortir un début de plan.

7 Construire le plan

1. Choisissez le plan qui vous paraît le plus approprié pour répondre à la problématique : *to what extent have civil actions help the fight against racial discrimination?*

a. I. An increased mobilisation
II. Legal actions
III. A wind of change

b. I. Helping fight racial discrimination
II. Not so efficient
III. Other ways?

c. I. Power of civil actions
II. Limits of civil actions

2. Écrivez 2 ou 3 idées pour chaque partie afin de développer votre plan.

OBJECTIF BAC

8 Rédiger la synthèse • Faire entendre sa voix

3 h

LE SUJET

D'après le travail préparatoire effectué dans les exercices 4 à 7, rédigez la synthèse sur le sujet proposé.

CORRIGÉS

SE TESTER QUIZ

1 Analyser un texte

1. a. an article • b. a speech • c. a novel
2. a. an editorial = personal opinion • b. news analysis = news • c. a review = personal opinion • d. news article = news

2 Analyser un graphe

a. 1962 • b. 1952 • c. 1954

3 Rédiger la synthèse

Phrases à cocher : a., b., c., g.

S'ENTRAÎNER

4 Analyser le sujet

1.

Civil actions	Qualities and purpose
petition / open letter	to raise awareness on an issue, argument and convince
city council / court actions	fight for justice, equal rights and treatments
demonstrations / marches	to show people's reactions, visibility
buzz on social media / street art	media and arts to shed light on issues, touch a vast majority of people

2. *Voici quelques exemples de problématiques possibles :* How can civil actions raise awareness on racial discrimination? To what extent have civil actions help the fight against racial discrimination? How powerful can civil actions be in fighting racial discrimination? What are effective ways to fight racial discrimination?

5 Lire le corpus

- Le document A est un article de presse paru dans le *New York Times* le 3 juillet 2020. Il présente Black Lives Matter comme le plus important mouvement contestataire moderne.
- Le document B est aussi un article, paru dans *The Guardian* le 3 novembre 2021. Il explique les enjeux du procès en lien avec le meurtre d'un jeune Afro-Américain dans l'État de Géorgie.
- L'œuvre de *street art* en noir et blanc (doc C), peinte sur les murs de New York, rend hommage aux Afro-Américains injustement tués ces dernières années.

6 Analyser et comparer l'apport de chaque document

1. et 2. Voici le tableau complété. On peut y repérer trois grandes idées : un mouvement sans précédent ; les conséquences ; un nouveau contexte impossible à nier.

Doc A	• BLM = the largest protest movement in US history • geographic spread / strong response to Trump's policy • white and young middle-class people mobilised. • Consequences: new laws and decisions across the country to fight racism. • An unprecedented movement that is changing American society • New wave and new state of mind.
Doc B	• George Floyd's trial and the conviction of the police officer + problematic Georgia law = repealed by the governor, yet still usable by the defence attorneys + jury selection issue. • Video footage: the jury and the judge cannot deny evidence anymore. • Legal actions allow social justice, equal rights and can reevaluate state laws that are unfair. • Black and white = the American society is racially divided + a call for blacks and whites to unite in this fight.
Doc C	• Steve "ESPO" Powers painted this piece: it displays the names of Black individuals who have lost their lives at the hands of police. • We can see the legs of people, but no face. The bold letters BLACK LIVES MATTER = the names are those of African-American people killed by racist acts. All the legs are moving in the same direction = a movement of solidarity. • Black and white mural = literal and figurative aspects. • The overwhelming number of names = a sense of despair, unfairness, and anger. • Art = a tool for capturing important moments in history like the Black Lives Matter.

7 Construire le plan

1. Réponse a. Les propositions b et c ne permettent pas d'apporter une réponse assez nuancée ("to what extent"), ou bien s'éloignent trop des documents.
2. *Voici une proposition pour détailler le plan.*

I. An increased mobilisation
- participants: numbers, background, geography...
- visibility

II. Legal actions
- Arbery's trial: guilty verdict
- changes in the law: examples all over the US (docs A and B)
- repairing a broken system

III. A wind of change
- a hopeful message from the three documents
- setting in motion undeniable proof

> **CONSEIL**
> Votre plan doit montrer une progression (des éléments les plus évidents aux éléments les plus implicites), afin d'éviter des contradictions au sein de votre synthèse. Donner des titres à vos parties sur votre brouillon vous aidera à regrouper vos idées de manière efficace.

OBJECTIF BAC

8 Rédiger la synthèse

Les titres en couleur et les puces permettent de mettre en évidence la structure du corrigé mais ils ne figureraient pas sur une copie de bac.

Introduction

The United States needs to face its racial issue head-on if they don't want to implode. Indeed, the Black Lives Matter that started after the murder of George Floyd by a Minneapolis police officer set up a wave of protests and awareness of racial divisions, tensions and discrimination. The three documents offer a vision of different actions taken to raise awareness on such a topical issue. So, to what extent have civil actions helped the fight against racial discrimination?

An increased mobilisation against racism

- The mural displayed in the streets of New York (C) is part of a worldwide campaign to support George Floyd and the Black Lives Matter movement. Displaying this in a public place where a majority of people can view it is a way to make this issue everyone's issue.
- Both documents A and C highlight the growing mobilisation of Americans in this issue. The demonstrations in 2020 peaked on July 6th. The article points out that the BLM movement is a landmark and a turning point as it is the biggest mobilisation of all times in the USA.
- Demonstrations all over the states and murals have reached a new part of the population (A): demonstrators are for the most part first-time demonstrators, they are younger and wealthier than in the past. This suggests a strong realisation that racial discrimination is a national matter.

Legal actions

■ **While** demonstrations and murals are playing an essential role in people's conscience, legal actions are attempting to bridge a gap and legally reduce racial discrimination.

CONSEIL
Les transitions permettent de passer subtilement d'une idée à l'autre.
Il faut faire le lien entre les idées qui se complètent dans cette synthèse.

■ George Floyd's murder by a police officer (mentioned in A) and the conviction of that police officer have opened new doors for racial justice. In this context, the guilty verdict of the three white men who murdered Ahmaud Arbery in Georgia (B) contribute to addressing the deeply rooted racial issue in the South and in the US more generally.

■ Not only are the verdicts in both cases setting a precedent, but they also point out the flaws of the legal system. The BLM movement (A) was born out of anger, despair and a strong feeling of injustice. The judicial branch (B) is now in the process of repairing those wrongdoings by sentencing the perpetrators of these crimes.

A wind of change

■ The three documents toy with both emotions (the unfair deaths of African-Americans) and a hopeful message that things are changing in the American society.

■ As Professor McAdam said, the BLM demonstrations set in motion a "significant, sustained, and widespread social, political change" (A). It is impossible now to turn a blind eye on this issue.

■ The media, the video footage, the murals are mediums and proof that racial discrimination cannot be ignored or rebutted any longer.

Conclusion

To conclude, the three documents prove that there is an awakening in American society and that racial discrimination has come to the forefront. Civil actions have started to pay off in this fight. Let's hope this will lead to a better future.

(498 words)

CONSEIL
La conclusion ne doit pas répéter mot pour mot des éléments de votre développement. C'est le moment de dresser le bilan et de donner une réponse claire à votre problématique. Il faut donc reformuler vos arguments de manière succincte puis offrir une ouverture qui élargit le sujet.

7 Améliorer son expression

La richesse de votre synthèse dépend en partie de votre capacité à utiliser un vocabulaire spécifique à l'AMC, des structures grammaticales plus complexes et à recourir à une palette d'expressions pour nuancer votre propos.

26 Bien organiser sa synthèse

En bref *Organiser sa synthèse est une phase essentielle de l'épreuve écrite. Vous allez devoir mettre en lien les documents en les comparant, en opérant des contrastes et des jeux de miroirs sous forme d'une expression écrite contenant les idées directrices des documents.*

I Rédiger l'introduction

1 Introduire le sujet

- La lecture du sujet est essentielle. Il faut veiller à bien cerner les **enjeux** des documents et repérer les éléments de **contexte** (actualité) et de **conceptualisation** (idée générale, représentation abstraite).
- L'**amorce** de votre devoir est cruciale car elle donne le ton de celui-ci. Préférez une phrase d'accroche (= quel·s enjeu·x le dossier soulève-t-il ?) puis présentez les documents et l'axe à l'aide de ce type de phrases :

  The documents under study / scrutiny are a… , a… and a…
  Within the framework of the topic "Puissance et influence", we…

2 Présenter les documents

L'introduction doit être le moment où vous **présentez les documents**. Précisez leur nature (carte, *cartoon*, article…), leur source (auteur, date, média) et le·s lien·s principal·aux au regard de la thématique et de l'axe du dossier.

The documents under study are an op-ed article from *The Guardian* published in 2020, a cartoon by Kevin Kallaughter and an article from *The New Yorker* published in 2021. They deal with the power and influence of the American Secret Service.

3 Proposer une problématique et un plan

- Dégagez votre problématique **qui va être le fil conducteur** de votre devoir. Ne pas confondre problème et problématique.

  Problème : There are a lot of cyberattacks nowadays in the USA.
  Problématique: What can the USA do to thwart cyberattacks? / To what extent is the fighting against cyberattacks crucial for the USA?

- **Annoncer votre plan** est une étape obligatoire, car il guide le ou la correcteur·trice et sert de colonne vertébrale.

  I will first focus on… I shall then… and lastly… I shall therefore deal with the evolution of the power and influence of the CIA worldwide and its new targets.

CONSEIL
Aérez votre copie en écrivant des paragraphes clairs, en faisant des alinéas à chaque étape de votre propos. N'oubliez pas de sauter une ligne entre l'introduction, le corps (1re et 2e parties) et la conclusion.

II Rédiger le développement

1 Organiser le corps du devoir

- Il n'y a pas de règle définie. Votre devoir doit suivre votre plan. Si vous annoncez deux ou trois parties dans votre introduction, il faudra bien les traiter.
- Chaque partie peut être composée de deux paragraphes.

CONSEIL
Mobilisez vos connaissances culturelles du monde anglophone pour enrichir votre analyse, mais ne les substituez pas au contenu du dossier.

2 Organiser ses paragraphes

Chaque paragraphe doit contenir une idée principale étayée par un exemple tiré des documents. Cela peut être le moment de présenter un élément de contraste → FICHE 27 tiré de l'un des deux autres documents. Enfin, utilisez un connecteur en début de paragraphe pour signaler que vous introduisez une nouvelle idée.

Introduire une idée	first, first of all, to begin with…
Ajouter des idées	secondly, thirdly…, then, afterwards, after that…, what is more, moreover, furthermore…
Conclure un paragraphe	to conclude, lastly, finally, eventually…

III Rédiger la conclusion

- Votre conclusion comprend deux moments :

– un résumé des idées principales que vous avez analysées dans votre synthèse puis une réponse claire à votre problématique ;

– une ouverture sur un autre aspect ou un autre axe de la thématique.

- Entamez votre conclusion avec une expression telle que *to conclude, in a nutshell, all in all, all things considered…*

zoOm

Faire référence à un document

L'essentiel est que votre source soit bien identifiée par l'examinateur.

> The article from *The Economist* shows how powerful … while document B encapsulates … . Indeeed, of the two documents, the latter seems more likely to depict the truth while the former is far from plausible. The best one that illustrates the topic is the document from the Pew Research Center.

Renvoyer au document…
- par sa nature
- selon sa source
- par son numéro ou sa lettre
- en le situant par rapport à un autre document

27 Muscler la logique interne de sa synthèse

En bref *La synthèse est un exercice d'argumentation. Vous devez être capable de lier vos idées avec des connecteurs (= mots de liaison) qui renforceront les divergences, les convergences et donc leur pertinence. En outre, il faudra éviter les propos univoques, mais plutôt adopter une posture nuancée.*

I Exprimer la comparaison

■ Pour mettre en lumière les différences entre les documents, plusieurs connecteurs ou expressions sont à votre disposition.

similarité	both / all three documents (*en début de phrase*), similarly... Document A is **as** + (*adjectif qualificatif*) + **as** the graph. Document A shows ... and **so does** the article.
opposition	while, although, conversely, contrary to document A which..., document B shows..., on the one hand, ... on the other hand...

Both documents B and C showcase the solidarity within specific US communities and amongst the Indian government that are trying to reduce the social and digital divides. Conversely, the graph doesn't give solutions, although it points out that American adults are also affected by this issue.

CONSEIL
Les documents expriment plusieurs idées qui peuvent converger ou diverger. Au brouillon, faites un tableau pour faire apparaître ces **oppositions ou similarités**.

II Exprimer la cause ou la conséquence

■ Lorsqu'on analyse un document, on doit comprendre son fonctionnement. Pour ce faire, on doit établir des liens de cause et de conséquence entre ce qui est dit ou montré dans le document et ce que l'on en déduit (= implicite).

■ Vous pouvez alors mettre en avant la cause (conjonctions, adverbes ou verbes) ou la conséquence (adverbes). Voici les principaux connecteurs ou expressions possibles.

cause	because, as, due to, on account of, insofar as, given that... blame so. for V-ing, accuse so. of V-ing, charge so with V-ing
conséquence	thus, in consequence, therefore, hence, consequently, so

The journalist blames the Republicans for helping affluent communities, therefore she urges local governments to act rapidly to help Karen Reyes's poorer students.

III Exprimer le but ou la condition

- Demandez-vous quels effets le document produit sur le lecteur. Montrez au correcteur que vous les avez relevés et expliquez leur·s rôle·s.
- Une fois que vous avez identifié le but poursuivi, introduisez-le par un connecteur exprimant la finalité comme *to, in order to, so as to, so (that) X can / could, for X to...*

  The Indian government is trying to find solutions **for** girls **to** be able to study in a safe environment *ou* ... **so that** girls **can** study...

- Vous pouvez également exprimer la condition grâce à des conjonctions comme *provided* et *unless*. Attention à leur construction.

  Girls **will** have more educational opportunities **provided** the government helps them.

  Girls will **not** have more educational opportunities **unless** the government helps them.

zoOm

Comment nuancer son propos ?

- Personne n'est vraiment dans la tête de l'auteur. Vous pouvez donc déduire ou émettre des hypothèses sur ce qu'il veut dire... ou alors sur un sens caché que vous aurez déduit. Pour cela il faut utiliser la modalité épistémique, c'est-à-dire la probabilité pour atténuer une affirmation, cela s'appelle le *hedging*.

au présent	au passé
Probabilité forte (j'en suis sûr) The journalist **must know** the truth.	**Probabilité forte** (must + have + participe passé) He **must have known** the truth.
Probabilité moyenne (je ne sais pas vraiment) The journalist **may know** the truth.	**Probabilité moyenne** (may + have + participe passé) He **may have known** the truth.
Probabilité faible (je n'en suis pas sûr, mais je le dis) The journalist **might know** the truth.	**Probabilité faible** (might + have + participe passé) He **might have known** the truth.

- Les adverbes, conjonctions ou expressions sont une autre manière de nuancer son propos.

Adverbes et conjonctions	Expressions
he **surely** means... • it is **often** said... he is **indisputably** the best... **however**, in the article... **nevertheless**... • **besides**... **though** (*en fin de phrase*)	the rate **tends to** decline... one must **acknowledge** that... actually, **on second thoughts**... **without any doubt**

28 Exploiter les documents spécifiques à l'AMC

En bref *Savoir mettre en valeur les documents qui composent les dossiers AMC (article, discours, graphiques, cartes...) grâce à un vocabulaire précis est un véritable atout qui vous permettra de faire la différence avec d'autres candidats et d'engranger des points dans le critère « richesse de la langue ».*

I Présenter un document

■ Lorsque vous présentez puis analysez un document, vous devez le désigner de manière appropriée.

Œuvres d'idées	an article, an essay, a speech, an op-ed (*tribune libre, débat d'idées*), a broadsheet, a tabloid, soft news, hard news
Œuvres visuelles	a photograph, a painting, an ad, a film poster, a cartoon
Documents statistiques	a graph, a table (*un tableau*), a chart or diagram a pie chart (*un graphique circulaire, un camembert*) a bar chart / graph (*un histogramme*) a map with key (*une carte avec légende*)
Œuvres de fiction	(an extract / excerpt from) a novel, a poem, a short story

✗ The set of documents is composed of document A by Adrienne Jones, document B from Pew Research Center and document C by Kevin Kallaughter.

✔ The set of documents is composed of an **op-ed article** by Adrienne Jones, a **graph** from Pew Research Center and a **cartoon** by Kevin Kallaughter.

■ L'auteur·e d'un document doit être clairement identifié·e : *columnist*, *journalist*, *cartoonist*, *photographer*, *computer graphics designer*, *novelist*, etc.

II Analyser un document

1 Décrire et analyser le contenu d'un document textuel

Nommer les parties d'un journal	front page, headline (*gros titre, manchette*), subheading (*sous-titre*), review (*critique*)
Traiter un thème	deal with, focus on, be about
Illustrer	illustrate my words, serve as an example, for instance
Représenter une idée, un concept	epitomise, embody, stand for, typify

Mettre l'accent, s'emparer d'une idée	highlight, underline, underscore, shed a light on, emphasise, pry into (*mettre son nez dans*), tackle the issue of (*s'attaquer au problème de*)
Reprendre une idée	echo, mirror, encapsulate, remind so. of

The article **encapsulates** the stereotyped image that American citizens have of their media, which **highlights** their distrust.

2 Décrire et analyser le contenu d'un document statistique

Décrire une évolution	plummet (*chuter fortement*), soar up (*augmenter fortement*), skyrocket (*grimper en flèche*) an increase, a rise, a decrease, a fall
Utiliser des données	forty percent, one third (1/3), two-third (2/3), a two-third majority

Public confidence in the UK government **plummeted** after Johnson's alleged parties.

3 Exprimer le point de vue de l'auteur

Juger une idée, un argument	libel (*diffamer*), enthral (*captiver*), yield (*céder*), bully (*harceler*), lambast (*descendre en flammes*)
Qualifier une idée, une attitude	biased (*partial*), accurate (*précis*), defiant (*réfractaire*), reliable (*fiable*), nonsensical (*qui n'a pas de sens*), unyielding (*inflexible*)

Democrats **lambasted** Republicans for distorting the truth.

zoOm

Décrypter les titres de la presse anglophone

Les titres des grands journaux anglophones sont parfois ardus à comprendre, car ils sont souvent elliptiques et fourmillent de références culturelles. Voyez plutôt :

NHS staff would rather celebrate 73rd birthday with a pay rise than with the George Cross

NHS → *National Health Service* (≈ Sécurité sociale britannique)

staff → employés

pay rise → augmentation de salaire

George Cross → la croix de Saint-Georges, distinction honorifique pour récompenser les civils.

→ Les employés de la Sécurité sociale britannique préféreraient fêter le 73e anniversaire (de l'institution) par une augmentation de salaire plutôt que par le titre honorifique de la croix de Saint-Georges (qui, donc, ne leur rapporte pas d'argent).

29 Varier et enrichir son expression

En bref *Pour apporter de la précision à votre argumentation et muscler les critères « richesse de la langue » (= vocabulaire) et « correction de la langue écrite » (= grammaire), il est indispensable de varier les mots et les structures grammaticales que vous utilisez.*

I Varier la construction de ses phrases

1 Utiliser la voie passive

Bien plus répandu en langue anglaise qu'en français, **le passif** permet de mettre en valeur le sujet qui subit l'action plutôt que celui qui fait l'action.

The journalist **published** his article "What About Going to the USA" on January 29, 2022.
→ "What About Going to the USA" **was published** on January 29, 2022.

2 Utiliser des structures complexes

Enrichir votre écrit par des **structures plus complexes** que celles apprises au collège ou en début de lycée vous permettra de faire la différence et d'apporter de la précision. En voici quelques exemples :

Structures « simples »	Structures complexes
Joe Biden should lift the ban.	**It's time** Joe Biden **lifted** the ban.
He agrees with the US President and the British Prime Minister.	**Not only does he agree** with the US President **but also** with the British Prime Minister.
When she speaks, people listen to her and are happy.	**The more** she speaks, **the happier** people are. (the more, the more)
I want Kamala Harris to become President of the USA.	I **wish** Kamala Harris **became / would become** President of the USA.
It is easy for Europe because it has the largest market of CO2 emission permits.	It is **all the** easier **as** Europe has the largest market of CO_2 emission permits.
The main reason for his failure is money.	It **all boils down to** money. (down to + V-ing)
The government really wants to help the poor.	The government **has committed to** help**ing** the poor.
If the Minister had known, he would have refused.	**Had** the Minister known, he **would** have refused.

II Employer un vocabulaire précis et varié

1 Utiliser des adjectifs efficaces et percutants

Lorsque vous évoquez un fait, une idée, une attitude, n'hésitez pas à le ou la qualifier. Bannissez *good, bad, important et interesting*.

⊕ striking, powerful, hard-hitting, inspired, bright, brilliant, intriguing, stimulating, fascinating, enthralling, gripping…

⊖ poor, harmful, evil, wicked, upsetting, defective, dreadful, awful, horrendous, appalling, ghastly, shady, ignorant

2 Utiliser des adverbes pour nuancer et préciser son propos

Certains adverbes permettent d'atténuer vos assertions ou d'apporter un complément de sens. L'adverbe se place avant le verbe sauf avec *be*.

atténuation	likely, unlikely, typically, rarely, often, sometimes
apport d'un complément	seemingly, repeatedly, in hindsight (*nom, avec du recul*), blindly, greatly, hopelessly
concession	though, however, yet, in spite of + V-ing, despite + V-ing
comparaison	as + adj. + as, less + adj. + than, less and less, more and more

zoOm

Se relire : les 5 règles clés

La relecture est capitale : vous devez vous assurer de la fluidité ainsi que de la correction orthographique et syntaxique de votre synthèse.

1. Corrigez les fautes d'inattention : -*s* à la 3e personne du singulier, *who* vs. *which*, verbe + COD (à ne pas séparer), orthographe des adverbes en -*ful*…
2. Ajoutez des connecteurs logiques pour lier vos phrases.
3. Ajoutez des modaux ou adverbes pour nuancer vos propos.
4. Renforcez votre écrit par des adjectifs percutants et des structures grammaticales complexes.
5. Remplacez les répétitions par des synonymes.

MÉMO VISUEL

AMÉLIORER

Organiser sa synthèse

Proposer une introduction
- Définir les termes importants de la **consigne**
- Présenter les **documents**
- Proposer un **plan** et une **problématique**

Rédiger un développement
- **Ordonner** les paragraphes
  → *first of all, secondly, lastly…*
- Organiser le **corps du devoir** (parties)

Formuler une conclusion
- Répondre à la **problématique** en lien avec l'axe
- Ouvrir la réflexion vers un **autre aspect** de l'axe

Utiliser des connecteurs logiques

Comparer les documents
- Faire **résonner** les documents entre eux
- Proposer des **contrastes** et des **similitudes**

Mettre en valeur un point de vue
- Montrer les **liens** entre les idées
- Montrer le **but de l'auteur** et **l'implicite** de ses propos

Faire preuve de nuance
- Apporter de la **nuance**
  → adverbes (*probably, surely*) et modaux (*must, might*)
- Connaître la **probabilité** au présent et au passé

Exploiter les documents spécifiques à l'AMC

Présenter les documents

- Savoir les **nommer** correctement
  → *op-ed, broadsheet, graph…*
- Désigner les auteurs
  → *columnist, cartoonist, photographer…*
- Être capable **de juger une idée**

Utiliser un lexique adéquat

- Maîtriser un lexique **spécifique**
  → *a graph, a chart, an article, an extract from an essay…*
- Parler d'une action, d'une évolution dans un **graphique**
- Parler du **ton** d'un texte d'idée
  → *denouncing, incisive, biased, unyielding…*

SON EXPRESSION

Varier et enrichir son expression

Varier la construction de ses phrases

- Utiliser la **voie passive** pour changer de point de vue
- Adopter des **structures complexes**
  → *not only…, all the more… as…*

Apporter de la précision

- Pimenter son propos avec des **adjectifs efficaces**
  → *enthralling, horrendous…*
- Enrichir ses phrases avec des **adverbes**
  → *hopelessly, unlikely…*

SE TESTER QUIZ

Vérifiez que vous avez bien compris les points clés des **fiches 26 à 29**.

1 Bien organiser sa synthèse

→ FICHE 26

1. Trouvez le synonyme des verbes suivants.

a. focus on •	• embody
b. illustrate my word •	• encapsulate
c. stand for •	• deal with
d. sum up •	• for instance

2. Corrigez l'orthographe et la syntaxe de ces phrases.

a. The journalist, in her article, ironicaly denounces the attack.

b. John Kerry speak very well French.

c. The idea, wich is horrendous, belongs at the former president Trump.

d. Puerto Rico has been colonise in 1508 by the Spanish.

2 Muscler la logique interne de sa synthèse

→ FICHE 27

Associez chaque phrase à l'intention suivante : cause, conséquence ou but.

a. The MP was excluded from the party for lying to the leader.

b. She went to Richmond in order to meet her British colleague.

c. He didn't have much time, so he asked for help.

d. G. W. Bush was heavily criticised for not telling the truth (about weapons of mass destruction).

3 Exploiter les documents spécifiques à l'AMC

→ FICHE 28

Faites correspondre chaque verbe à son synonyme.

a. libel •	• captivate
b. lambast •	• accept
c. enthral •	• publish false information
d. yield •	• attack verbally

4 Varier et enrichir son expression

→ FICHE 29

Remplacez les *good* et *bad* par des adjectifs plus précis.

I have read a good article about a good policy that is going to forbid bad political leaders to run for office. That's a good piece of news! At least, I hope bad voters will stop voting for these kinds of bad politicians.

S'ENTRAÎNER

5 Rédiger dans un anglais correct

→ FICHE 29

Voici un extrait d'une copie d'élève. Pointez les erreurs (temps des verbes, ordre des mots, orthographe, sens…) puis effectuez les corrections.

After the World war one and the world war two, a huge part of puerto Ricans went to USA. Today, there are around three millions persons in the island and more that five in USA mainland, and more particulary in New York. In 1958 was the first parade of puerto rican in this city. It is late, it show how is their culture important.

6 Comprendre la similarité et l'opposition

→ FICHE 27

1. **Repérez la similarité et l'opposition, puis surlignez les connecteurs logiques.**

similarité	opposition

All three documents focus on online education. Similarly, the two articles highlight the widening social and class gap. Indeed, both articles point at the inequities that exist and that have become more apparent with online education. However, the graph doesn't really propose solutions.

2. **Reformulez les énoncés en utilisant les amorces fournies.**

a. Democrats have blamed Republicans because they didn't reach an agreement.
→ *Democrats have blamed Republicans for…*

b. Lawyers have accused the police. They beat Ronald Greene to death.
→ *Lawyers have accused the police of…*

c. I think I did all right. I didn't study much for the test.
→ *I think I did all right given…*

d. The burglar was charged. He stole four expensive watches.
→ *The burglar was charged…*

CONSEILS
Les amorces proposées pour les reformulations vont entraîner des modifications des formes verbales, par exemple.

7 Apporter une nuance en complexifiant

→ FICHE 29

Reformulez ces énoncés en les complexifiant avec les aides proposées et en effectuant les changements appropriés.

a. The journalist is certain that it is more difficult for Indian girls to have access to a quality education.
→ *It / must / for / Indian girls / have access / according to / journalist*

b. I'm sure, the rioters were charged because they barged into the Capitol.
→ *The rioters / must / charged / barge into / Capitol*

c. She belongs to the Labour Party, but I really don't know.
→ *She / {modal} / Labour Party*

d. If he had been to the club, then I'm sure he saw her.
→ *If he had been to the club / then / he / {modal} / see / her*

e. The lock is broken. I'm sure that someone broke into the house.
→ *The lock is broken, someone / {modal} / break into the house*

8 Utiliser des structures complexes

→ FICHE 29

Reformulez ces énoncés en les complexifiant avec les amorces fournies.

a. I'm not mad at you because you left the meeting. → *blame*

b. Nurses want a pay increase and reduced hours. → *not only*

c. A convicted felon was prosecuted. He murdered a police officer. → *charge*

d. When I see you, I am always happy. → *the more, the more*

e. I really wanted to work on this project for the next 6 months. → *commit to*

OBJECTIF BAC

9 Créer du sens

Utilisez les mots de liaison suivants pour que le texte retrouve du sens.

unlike • according to • as • while • somehow • in a nutshell • surprisingly enough

.... crowd-counting experts, around 20 million Americans have participated in demonstrations over the death of George Floyd. .... it is possible for marchers to answer twice, it is .... the largest movement in US history. However, ... with past Black Lives Matter, nearly 95% of US counties that had a protest are majority white. ...., the protests are colliding with a watershed moment: the country's most devastating pandemic. .... people have been stuck at home, they now need to express more their anger, their sadness or .... their desire to make this world a better place.

CORRIGÉS

SE TESTER QUIZ

1 Bien organiser sa synthèse

1. a. focus on: deal with • **b.** illustrate my word: for instance • **c.** stand for: embody • **d.** sum up: encapsulate

2. a. In her article, the journalist ironically denounces the attack.
b. John Kerry speaks French very well.
c. The idea, which is horrendous, belongs to former President Trump.
d. Puerto Rico was colonised in 1508 by the Spaniards.

2 Muscler la logique interne de sa synthèse

a. cause : for lying. *For + V-ing* exprime la cause.
b. but : in order to. *In order to* + BV exprime le but.
c. conséquence : so. *So* relie deux membres de phrase et exprime la conséquence.
d. cause : for not telling. *For + V-ing* exprime la cause (ici négative).

> **INFO**
> À la place de ***in order to*** on peut lier deux membres de phrases avec ***so as to***.

3 Exploiter les documents spécifiques à l'AMC

a. libel: publish false information (*diffamer*)
b. lambast: attack verbally (*descendre en flèche*)
c. enthral: captivate
d. yield: accept (*céder*)

4 Varier et enrichir son expression

Proposition possible :
I have read a surprising article about an effective policy that is going to forbid dishonest political leaders to run for office. That's a great piece of news! At least, I hope careless voters will stop voting for these kinds of crooked politicians.

S'ENTRAÎNER

5 Rédiger dans un anglais correct

After ~~the~~ World War I and ~~the~~ World War II, a huge part of Puerto Ricans went to the USA. Today, there are around three million**s** ~~persons~~ inhabitants / people ~~in~~ on the island and more ~~that~~ than five million live in the USA mainland, and more particularly in New York. In 1958, they decided to hold the first Puerto Rican Day Parade in this city. Even if it may be late, it shows how ~~is their culture important~~ important their unique culture is.

> **CONSEIL**
> Après *New York*, on aurait pu faire apparaître un lien cause-conséquence : *As they were numerous / As they formed a new diaspora, they decided to hold...*

6 Comprendre la similarité et l'opposition

similarité	opposition

1. All three documents focus on online education. Similarly, the two articles highlight the widening social and class gap. Indeed, both articles point at the inequities that exist and that have become more apparent with online education. However, the graph doesn't really propose solutions.

2. a. Democrats have blamed Republicans for not reaching an agreement.
b. Lawyers have accused the police of beating Ronald Greene to death.
c. I think I did all right given that I didn't study much for the test.
d. The burglar was charged with stealing four expensive watches.

7 Apporter une nuance en complexifiant

a. It **must be** more difficult **for** Indians girls **to** have access to a quality education, according to the journalist.
b. The rioters **must have been charged with** barg**ing** into the Capitol.
c. She **might / may** belong to the Labour Party.
d. If she had been to the club, then, he **must have seen** her.
e. The lock is broken, someone **must have broken** into the house.

CONSEIL
Les modaux ***may*** et ***might*** peuvent aussi servir à exprimer une probabilité future plus (*may*) ou moins (*might*) certaine : *Kamala Harris might become US next President in 2024.*

8 Utiliser des structures complexes

a. I don't **blame** you / I'm not **blaming** you **for** leav**ing** the meeting.
b. **Not only do** nurses want a pay increase **but also** reduced hours.
c. A convicted felon was **charged with** murder**ing** a police officer.
d. **The more** I see you, **the** happi**er** I am.
e. I **committed to** work**ing** on the project for the next 6 months.

OBJECTIF BAC

9 Créer du sens

According to crowd-counting experts, around 20 million Americans have participated in demonstrations over the death of George Floyd. **While** it is possible for marchers to answer twice, it is **somehow** the largest movement in US history. However, **unlike** with past Black Lives Matter, nearly 95% of US counties that had a protest are majority white. **Surprisingly enough**, the protests are colliding with a watershed moment: the country's most devastating pandemic. **As** people have been stuck at home, they now need to express more their anger, their sadness or **in a nutshell** their desire to make this world a better place.

CONSEIL
Lorsque vous rédigez un paragraphe, l'essentiel est bien la manière dont vous développez des idées, en revanche savoir les articuler avec des connecteurs logiques est un plus.

8 Traduire ou transposer un texte

Nul besoin d'être un expert en linguistique pour réussir la traduction : il faut considérer l'exercice comme un puzzle où chaque pièce trouve sa place.

* Il fallait traduire : Angela a commencé à pleurer à cause de la douleur, elle doit encore se remettre de sa blessure.

30 Se lancer dans une traduction

En bref *La version (traduction de l'anglais vers le français) a un double objectif : tester la compréhension de la langue source mais aussi la maîtrise de la langue cible. Cet exercice rigoureux requiert une démarche spécifique en plusieurs étapes.*

I La procédure générale

1 Aborder le passage

- Relisez le texte puis le passage à traduire attentivement. La version doit faire suite à l'analyse du texte qui a permis une **compréhension fine** de celui-ci et de ses caractéristiques.
- Repérez la nature du passage, les personnages, leurs rapports, le ou les lieux, l'époque, les événements, **le point de vue, le ton et le niveau de langue**.
- Délimitez les **unités de sens** avant de commencer.

  To the European settlers | the whole province | looked like | a barbaric place | inhabited by | appalling terrifying bloodthirsty savages.

MOT CLÉ
Unité de sens : mots ou groupes de mots pertinents du point de vue de la syntaxe et du lexique.

2 Traduire

Il s'agit de **restituer le sens d'origine** en tenant compte des spécificités linguistiques et culturelles de chacune des deux langues ainsi que des particularités inhérentes au texte d'origine.

Les 4 règles clés

1. **Commencez par une traduction littérale** (ou mot à mot).
2. **Affinez la traduction** en utilisant des procédés de traduction → FICHE 32, en cherchant à trouver le mot juste, l'expression adéquate.
3. **Rédigez dans un français authentique** rendant compte du style et du niveau de langue du texte source.
4. **Relisez la traduction** pour vous assurer que le sens du message est clair en français. Puis relisez parallèlement le texte en anglais et la traduction pour vérifier que rien n'a été omis.

II Conseils pratiques

1 **Évitez le recours systématique au dictionnaire** : il est parfois possible de surmonter autrement les difficultés lexicales. → FICHE 31

2 **Évitez le mot à mot systématique** : il faut tenir compte de l'ordre canonique de la phrase et respecter les conventions propres à chaque langue : succession des adjectifs, place des compléments circonstanciels…

Caitrin is a beautiful talented Irish woman who lives with her grumpy old uncle in a tiny flat in London.

✗ Caitrin est une femme irlandaise belle et talentueuse qui vit avec son oncle vieux et grincheux dans un minuscule appartement à Londres.

✔ Caitrin est une belle Irlandaise talentueuse qui vit à Londres dans un minuscule appartement avec son vieil oncle grincheux.

3 **Tenez compte des conventions d'écriture** : emploi des signes de ponctuation, utilisation des majuscules ou minuscules.

She loves Irish music, just like her secret admirer.

✔ Elle adore la musique irlandaise, tout comme son admirateur secret.

4 **Veillez à la correction de la langue cible** (grammaire, syntaxe et orthographe) : une langue fautive est sanctionnée même si la traduction montre une bonne compréhension du texte. Attention au passé simple notamment et au franglais !

The old lady in charge of her musical education was so exhausted and downhearted that she sat down on the damp grass.

✗ La vieille femme en charge de [*franglais*] son éducation musicale était si épuisé et découragé [*accord*] qu'elle s'asseya [*conjugaison, barbarisme*] sur l'herbe mouillée.

zoom

Sur-traduire ou sous-traduire

Il convient de vérifier que l'on n'a ni **sous-traduit** ni au contraire **sur-traduit**, ce qui induirait soit une perte au niveau du message soit une interprétation plutôt qu'une traduction.

Sous-traduction (bleu)	Sur-traduction (vert)

She fondly dwelt on her long-gone glorious past as a grand piano player: her career had taken her abroad to Switzerland, Italy and Russia.

→ Elle pensait tendrement à son ancienne carrière glorieuse de grande pianiste : ses tournées de plus en plus nombreuses l'avaient amenée à se produire partout en Europe, en particulier en Suisse, en Italie et en Russie.

31 Traduire le lexique

En bref *La version est un exercice de précision qui requiert une bonne connaissance du lexique dans les deux langues. Face à des mots ou expressions inconnus, il faut adopter plusieurs stratégies pour aboutir à une traduction juste : inférer dans un premier temps le sens des mots puis utiliser le dictionnaire unilingue.*

I Utiliser le contexte et ses connaissances

- Utiliser le contexte et identifier la **nature** et la **fonction grammaticale** du lexique inconnu permet d'accéder au sens et d'envisager une première traduction qu'il faudra peut-être affiner selon le cas.

  She has become a grumpy old lady and she keeps complaining and whining, she finds fault in everything.

  La forme et place du mot indiquent qu'il s'agit d'un verbe et le contexte permet d'en déduire qu'il a un sens proche de *complain* (se plaindre) donc ***whine*** **= geindre**.

- Pour avoir un solide bagage lexical, il convient d'apprendre le lexique régulièrement et d'enrichir ses connaissances de **synonymes** et **expressions idiomatiques**. Cela permet ensuite de repérer rapidement les mots transparents et les faux amis.

  sympathetic → compréhensif, compatissant
  eventually → finalement
  sensible → raisonnable

II Analyser la formation des mots

- Maîtriser les procédés de **dérivation**, c'est-à-dire comment se forment les mots, permet de retrouver le mot racine et ainsi, en fonction des **suffixes et préfixes** repérés, d'**inférer** le sens des mots inconnus.

  carefully = *care* + *ful* = adj. + *ly* = adv.
  → soigneusement
  unfriendly = *un* + *friend* + *ly* = adj.
  → hostile, déplaisant

À NOTER
L'ajout de **préfixes** a un impact direct sur le sens du mot alors que l'ajout de **suffixes** change aussi la catégorie grammaticale de celui-ci.

- Connaître la **règle de composition** permet de traduire convenablement les mots composés, qu'il s'agisse d'adjectifs ou de noms. En anglais, le mot qui se trouve en dernière position porte le sens principal et le mot qui se trouve en position initiale permet de préciser celui-ci.

  homemade → fait maison
  horserace → course de chevaux
  racehorse → cheval de course

zoom

Comment utiliser le dictionnaire unilingue ?

Yet, Caitrin couldn't blame her for the old lady's mood swings and helplessness reminded her of her beloved uncle.

- Identifier la racine du mot ou du moins débarrasser le mot inconnu de tous les marqueurs grammaticaux tels que la marque du pluriel ou encore les modifications verbales (V-*ing*, prétérit, participe passé) permet de rendre la recherche plus efficace.

helplessness = ***help*** + *less* + *ness*

- Déterminer la catégorie grammaticale des mots inconnus permet de s'intéresser directement à la bonne proposition dans le cas où un même mot aurait plusieurs natures.

helplessness = nom car adjectif + suffixe *ness*. *Help* est ici un nom en raison des règles de dérivation : le suffixe *less* se rajoute toujours à un nom pour former un adjectif.

help[2] *n* **1** [U] the act of helping; AID; ASSISTANCE: *You're not (of) much help to me just sitting there. | You gave me a lot of help* **2** [C (*to*)] something or somebody that helps: *You're a good help to me. | The new fire is a great help* **3** [U *nonassertive*] a way of avoiding (esp. in the phr. **no help for it**) **4** [C] a person, esp. female, who is employed to do some of someone else's housework: *The new help left after a week* **5** [P] esp. AmE workers, esp. female house servants: *The help are demanding higher wages* **6 Help! a** Please bring help, I'm in danger **b** (an expression of surprise and inability to act) **7 Help Wanted** (a sign offering employment)

Polysémie : lire l'article en entier avant de choisir la définition qui convient en fonction du contexte.

Caractéristiques : repérer si le mot est dénombrable (C pour *countable*) ou indénombrable (U pour *uncountable*) et où il est utilisé (AmE = American English par exemple). Le niveau de langue peut être précisé (fml = soutenu, lit = littéraire, coll / infml = familier, sl = argot).

Synonymes : ils peuvent permettre de trouver une traduction adéquate.

Exemples : ils orientent la compréhension et la traduction en donnant un contexte d'emploi.

Expressions idiomatiques ou collocations, expressions figées.

→ Pourtant, Caitrin ne pouvait lui en vouloir car les sautes d'humeur et la détresse de la vieille dame lui rappelaient son oncle bien aimé.

32 Utiliser les procédés de traduction

En bref *Toute traduction passe nécessairement par l'utilisation de procédés de traduction. Il convient de distinguer les procédés directs de traduction qui sont utilisés lors du premier jet et les procédés indirects de traduction qui permettent d'affiner ce premier jet souvent maladroit, fautif, voire incompréhensible en français.*

I Les procédés directs

1 La traduction littérale

Il s'agit d'une version **mot à mot** qui reste au plus près du texte de départ, avec le minimum de transformations nécessaires. Si la structure syntaxique de l'énoncé est la même dans les deux langues, on se concentre sur le lexique, les déterminants et les formes verbales.

She had only found fault with her right from the start and it had nothing to do with her so-called gift: she disapproved of both her manners and her gait.

Elle ne lui avait trouvé que des défauts dès le début et cela n'avait rien à voir avec son soi-disant don : elle n'approuvait ni ses manières ni son allure.

2 L'emprunt

- L'emprunt consiste à **importer dans la langue cible** un mot ou une expression de la langue source, c'est-à-dire à employer le mot ou l'expression tels quels.
- Il permet de combler une lacune culturelle ou linguistique :

  coroner, sheriff, pub
- de faire « couleur locale » :

  hello (pour *bonjour*)
- de simplifier la phrase, notamment quand le terme est plus court :

  hacker, sniper

3 Le calque

- Les calques sont toujours fautifs, même si certains sont entrés dans l'usage. Il s'agit de traduire un mot ou une expression en important dans la langue cible une structure propre à la langue source dans le cas du **calque de structure** :

  for discussion → pour discussion

  (maintenant acceptable en français, même si c'est un anglicisme – à la place de *pour qu'on en discute*, qui est la tournure naturelle en français)
- Le calque permet aussi d'employer en français un mot ou une expression qui n'a pas le même sens que celui recherché dans le cas du **calque d'expression** :

  Secretary of State → secrétaire d'État (au lieu de *ministre des Affaires étrangères*)

II Les procédés indirects

1 La transposition

- La **transposition** consiste à opérer un changement de catégorie grammaticale sans modifier le message, par exemple du nom au verbe, de l'adjectif au nom.

  Diamonds are Forever → Les diamants sont éternels

> **HELP**
> À ne pas confondre avec l'exercice de transposition. → FICHE 34

- Il y a deux cas particuliers de transposition : l'étoffement quand on remplace un mot par plusieurs, et le chassé-croisé quand on permute les éléments signifiants.

  He ran across the lawn. → Il a traversé la pelouse en courant.

2 L'équivalence

- L'équivalence consiste à remplacer une formule plus ou moins figée de la langue source par une autre, équivalente dans la langue cible. Elle est utilisée pour les expressions idiomatiques, proverbes, panneaux de signalisation, etc.

  You're welcome. (en réponse à *thank you*) → Il n'y a pas de quoi. / Avec plaisir.

- L'adaptation est rattachée à une situation donnée ou à l'arrière-plan culturel. On s'en sert pour les dialectes, jargons, jeux de mots notamment mais aussi pour les unités de mesure : gallons → litres avec conversion.

3 La modulation

Elle opère un changement de point de vue au niveau du message. Mais le sens global est conservé. Ce changement engendre un glissement d'ordre lexical ou d'ordre grammatical.

English spoken → ici, on parle anglais   quite maliciously → non sans malice

zoOm

Les titres d'œuvres

Ils doivent être accrocheurs et peuvent parfois être très surprenants.

Mot à mot	*The Fifth Element*	*Le Cinquième Élément*
Transposition	*Star Wars*	*La Guerre des étoiles*
Modulation	*Rabbit-Proof Fence*	*Le Chemin de la liberté*
Modulation et transposition	*Dangerous Minds* *Viceroy's House*	*Esprits rebelles* *Le Dernier Vice-Roi des Indes*
Équivalence	*From Russia with Love*	*Bons Baisers de Russie*
Choix d'un titre (pseudo) anglais	*Night Crawler* *The Post*	*Night Call* *Pentagon Papers*

33 Résoudre les problèmes de traduction

En bref *Les problèmes de traduction sont liés aux spécificités des deux systèmes linguistiques. Les problèmes d'ordre grammatical concernent les groupes nominal et verbal ainsi que la phrase et nécessitent la combinaison de plusieurs procédés de traduction.*

I Les groupes nominal et verbal

1 Le groupe nominal

- L'emploi des **déterminants** (article et possessifs) peut être différent.
  John's mother is *a* nurse. → La mère de John est Ø infirmière.
  He had *his* hands in *his* pockets. → Il avait *les* mains dans *les* poches.
- Les **adjectifs** décrivant une relation entre le nom et un autre élément ne se traduisent pas par des adjectifs.
  medical student → un étudiant *en médecine*

Il faut faire attention à **l'ordre des adjectifs** dans le cas d'une suite d'adjectifs.

À NOTER
Avant un nom, *beau, joli, bon* précèdent les autres adjectifs. **Après un nom**, les adjectifs les plus généraux sont devant et les participes passés à la fin.

- Les **pronoms possessifs** peuvent se traduire par des adjectifs possessifs.
  John is a friend of *mine*. → John est un de *mes* amis.

2 Le groupe verbal

Structure grammaticale	Choix de traduction	Exemple
Passif	Voix active	He *was given* a book yesterday. → *On lui a donné* un livre hier.
Modaux	Adverbes	He *must* be a policeman. → Il est *très certainement* policier.
Formes en *-ing*	Différemment selon leur fonction	Smoking is forbidden. → Il est interdit de fumer. I am warning you. → C'est un avertissement.
Reprise par auxiliaire	Sans l'auxiliaire	I didn't know about it. *Did you?* → Je n'étais pas au courant. *Et toi ?*
Verbes à particule	Dans certains cas, chassé-croisé	I'll ride back. → Je rentrerai en vélo. He ran into the room. → Il est entré dans la pièce en courant.

II La phrase

1 Structures causatives et résultatives

- Les **structures causatives** sont traduites selon le même modèle : il s'agit de faire faire quelque chose, éventuellement à quelqu'un.

  He made me do it again. → Il m'a fait recommencer.

  He had the wall painted. → Il a fait peindre le mur.

- Les **structures résultatives** mettent l'accent sur le résultat d'une action et le moyen pour l'obtenir. Elles s'utilisent donc pour convaincre ou persuader.

  He talked him out of driving. → Il l'a dissuadé de conduire.

Elles peuvent aussi signifier un changement de lieu ou d'état.

I ate myself sick. → Je me suis rendu malade à force de manger.

2 Relatives et ponctuation

- Dans le cas d'une **relative déterminative**, donc sans virgule, il peut être nécessaire d'étoffer.

  My sister who is a model is in Leeds. → Celle de mes sœurs qui est mannequin est à Leeds.

- Dans le cas d'une **relative non déterminative**, on traduit en respectant la ponctuation.

  My sister, who is a model, is in Leeds.

  → Ma sœur, qui est mannequin, est à Leeds.

À NOTER

Une **relative déterminative** est nécessaire à la compréhension du message alors qu'une **relative non déterminative** apporte une information supplémentaire.

zoOm

Comprendre la correction de sa copie

En plus des erreurs de français, les erreurs de traduction sont signalées par des termes précis.

Type d'erreur	Définition
Faux-sens	Prendre un mot pour un autre. Traduire *sparrow* (moineau) par « hirondelle ».
Contresens	Faux-sens aggravé montrant que l'on n'a pas compris. Traduire *sparrow* par « flèche » (*arrow*).
Non-sens	Texte absurde ou incohérent dans la langue cible.
Omission	Oubli considéré comme un abandon ou un refus de traduire face à la difficulté.
Syntaxe	Erreurs dans l'ordre des mots, pouvant aller jusqu'à construire une syntaxe qui n'existe pas dans la langue.
Temps	Erreur de choix de temps ou de forme verbale.

34 Réussir un exercice de transposition

En bref *L'exercice de transposition ne consiste pas à traduire un texte mot à mot, mais à rendre compte en français des idées et arguments qui y sont développés, en les explicitant si besoin. Pour cela, vous devez d'abord bien comprendre et analyser le texte source.*

I Comprendre et analyser le texte

1 Identifier texte et contexte

- Tout d'abord, étudiez les éléments du paratexte (titre, auteur, source, date de publication). Cela permet d'inscrire ce document dans son contexte (social, politique, historique, etc.). Puis relisez le texte afin d'identifier les mots et thèmes clés.
- Repérez les idées du texte qu'il vous paraît pertinent d'expliciter.

2 Dégager idées principales et structure

- Le travail d'analyse consiste ensuite à dégager les idées principales en repérant les différents arguments développés. Il est impératif de bien distinguer l'argument (que vous conserverez pour en rendre compte dans la transposition) de l'exemple (qui relève du détail et que vous ne garderez pas).
- Il s'agit également de repérer la structure du texte. Pour cela, surlignez tous les connecteurs logiques qui indiquent les mouvements du texte : contrastes et similarités (*however*, *alike*, *similarly*...), comparaisons, etc.

3 Repérer point de vue et intention

- Enfin l'analyse requiert aussi d'identifier le point de vue et l'intention de l'énonciateur. L'auteur cherche-t-il à persuader, conseiller, décrire ou informer ? Adopte-t-il un ton polémique, humoristique ou ironique ?
- À l'issue de cette première étape, vous aurez ainsi clairement défini la structure argumentative, les idées majeures défendues dans le texte et les éléments à expliciter.

II Rédiger le compte rendu en français

1 Écrire le compte rendu

- Utilisez les éléments de l'analyse pour rendre compte en français de l'essentiel du texte de manière claire, nouvelle et personnelle. Il est cependant primordial de rester fidèle aux propos de l'auteur. Vous devez aussi respecter la structure argumentative du texte initial.

REMARQUE
On trouve généralement une idée par paragraphe.

- Il semble raisonnable de ne pas aller au-delà de 150 mots environ même quand cela n'est pas précisé dans le sujet. Vous devez respecter les contraintes de longueur si elles sont données.

2 Relire le compte rendu

- Relisez une première fois votre compte rendu pour vérifier le contenu et vous assurer que les idées majeures sont restituées dans l'ordre et articulées selon la même logique que le texte source.
- Enfin, vous devez relire attentivement votre compte rendu une seconde fois pour contrôler la langue et vous assurer que l'orthographe, la grammaire et la ponctuation sont corrects.

zoOm

Identifier la structure d'un texte

Les connecteurs logiques articulent le texte et servent à établir une relation entre les opinions et arguments avancés.

Idée exprimée	English expressions or link words
addition (et, de même que, encore...)	moreover, in addition, furthermore, not only... but also, besides, likewise, similarly
opposition (mais, bien que, cependant, malgré...)	although, even though, though, nonetheless, nevertheless, however, and yet, still, by contrast, conversely
cause (comme, effectivement, grâce à...)	since, as, because of, thanks to, due to, owing to
conséquence (donc, de sorte que, c'est pourquoi...)	thus, so that, that's why, as a consequence, consequently, as a result, therefore, so + adj. ... that, such + GN ... that
exemple (par exemple, c'est-à-dire, en d'autres termes...)	for instance, for example, that is to say, namely, in other words
but (pour, afin de, dans le but de...)	to, in order to, so as to, with the aim of, so that + may
supposition (si, en cas de...)	whether, if, should there be
conclusion (finalement, en définitive, en dernier lieu...)	finally, ultimately, lastly, eventually

RÉUSSIR SA TRADUCTION OU SA TRANSPOSITION

3 Relire sa copie

La traduction

- **Relisez le texte en français**
  - Assurez-vous que le **message** est clair et compréhensible
  - Vérifiez que la **langue** est correcte
- **Relisez la traduction et le texte original en même temps**
  - Assurez-vous que vous avez **réellement traduit** (et non interprété) le texte original
  - Vérifiez qu'il n'y a aucune **omission**

La transposition

- **Relisez le texte en français**
  - Assurez-vous que le **message** est clair et compréhensible
  - Vérifiez que la **langue** est correcte
- **Relisez la transposition et le texte original en même temps**
  - **Comparez** le texte original et votre transposition
  - Assurez-vous que vous avez bien respecté l'**ordre** des arguments

1 Aborder l'exercice

La traduction

- **Lisez** le texte attentivement
- **Analysez**-le et repérez les unités de sens
- **Inférez** le sens des mots inconnus
- Si nécessaire, utilisez le **dictionnaire unilingue**

La transposition

- **Lisez** le texte attentivement
- **Analysez**-le et repérez les **idées principales**
- Distinguez arguments et exemples (ne gardez que les **arguments**)

2 Réaliser l'exercice

La traduction : proposer un texte qui sonne juste en français

- Lorsque c'est nécessaire, modifiez :
  - la catégorie grammaticale **(transposition)**
  - le point de vue **(modulation)**
  - une expression typique **(équivalence)**
- Prenez en compte les spécificités des deux langues
- Prêtez attention aux **temps des verbes**, à l'ordre des mots et au **niveau de langue**

La transposition : rédiger un compte rendu en français

- Repérez la **structure** argumentative du texte
- Rédigez votre compte rendu en français en suivant l'**ordre du texte initial**

SE TESTER QUIZ

Vérifiez que vous avez bien compris les points clés des **fiches 31 à 33**.

1 Traduire le lexique

→ FICHE 31

1. Associez chaque expression au niveau de langue employé.

a. annoyed •	• formal
b. pissed off •	• informal
c. discontented •	• vulgar

2. Traduisez par des procédés de dérivation et selon la composition.

a. an unforgettable creepy-crawler → ....

b. admiring cave-drawings → ....

c. unobtainable records → ....

2 Utiliser les procédés de traduction

→ FICHE 32

Vrai ou faux ? Cochez la case qui convient.	V	F
a. On traduit les verbes à particules à l'aide du chassé-croisé.	☐	☐
b. La transposition opère un changement de point de vue.	☐	☐
c. On ne peut traduire les expressions idiomatiques et les proverbes.	☐	☐
d. Le calque est une traduction littérale souvent fautive.	☐	☐

3 Résoudre les problèmes de traduction

→ FICHE 33

Cochez la traduction qui convient.

1. Paula's and John's parents talked them into staying.

☐ a. Les parents de Paula et ceux de John leur ont parlé de rester.
☐ b. Les parents de Paula et ceux de John les ont convaincus de rester.
☐ c. Les parents de Paula et John les ont persuadés de rester.

2. He had had different jobs. And all the while he studied and read.

☐ a. Il avait eu divers emplois. Et, durant tout ce temps, il étudiait et il lisait.
☐ b. Il avait eu divers emplois. Et, durant tout ce temps, il étudia et il lut.
☐ c. Il eut divers emplois. Et, durant tout ce temps, il avait étudié et lu.

3. He had been on the sofa ever since he'd lost his job.

☐ a. Il avait passé son temps sur le canapé depuis qu'il avait perdu son travail.
☐ b. Il passait son temps sur le canapé depuis qu'il avait perdu son travail.
☐ c. Il a passé son temps sur le canapé depuis qu'il a perdu son travail.

S'ENTRAÎNER

4 La transposition et la modulation

→ FICHE 32

Traduisez les phrases suivantes en utilisant les procédés adaptés.

a. He eventually staggered into the lifeboat.

→ ....

b. Her nails definitely need attention.

→ ....

c. A Mrs Jones keeps ringing.

→ ....

d. Don't forget to pick up the kids!

→ ....

CONSEIL
N'hésitez pas à utiliser plusieurs procédés dans une même phrase.

5 L'équivalence

→ FICHE 32

Associez chaque expression à son équivalent.

a. I smell a rat. •	• Ça coûte les yeux de la tête.
b. Mind the gap. •	• Ils se vendent comme des petits pains.
c. They are selling like hot cakes. •	• Il y a anguille sous roche.
d. It costs the earth. •	• Attention à la marche.

6 L'emploi des déterminants

→ FICHE 33

Complétez les phrases suivantes avec les déterminants qui conviennent.

a. He promised freedom to his slave.

→ Il promit .... liberté à son esclave.

b. She's cut her finger while preparing dinner.

→ Elle s'est coupé .... doigt alors qu'elle préparait le dîner.

c. When I was a child, I used to dress up as a pirate.

→ Lorsque j'étais .... enfant, je me déguisais en .... pirate.

7 La voix passive et la voix active

→ FICHE 33

She was engrossed in English literature. She was said to be a bookworm and was learned indeed. Yet, the Romantics eluded her until she was offered Wordsworth's *Lyrical Ballads*. She quickly read them all and was thus turned into a Romantic herself.

1. Avec deux couleurs différentes, soulignez les différents types de verbes :

verbes à la voix passive	verbes à la voix active

2. Traduisez le texte en choisissant la voix qui convient.

OBJECTIF BAC

8 Traduction en français

→ FICHES 31 à 33

Traduisez le passage suivant en français.

Miss Lucy tells the students of Hailsham, the boarding school where she works, about their prospects for the future.

"The problem, as I see it, is that you've been told and not told. You've been told, but none of you really understand, and I dare say, some people are quite happy to leave it that way. But I'm not. If you're going to have decent lives, then you've got to know and know properly. None of you will go to America, none of you will be film stars. [...] Your lives are set out for you. You'll become adults, then before you're old, before you're even middle-aged, you'll start to donate your vital organs. That's what each of you was created to do."

Kazuo Ishiguro, *Never Let Me Go*,
© Faber & Faber, 2005.

9 Transposition

→ FICHE 34

Rendez compte en français des principales idées exprimées par le document.

This election had many firsts and many stories that will be told for generations. But one that's on my mind tonight's about a woman who cast her ballot in Atlanta. [...] Ann Nixon Cooper is 106 years old. She was born just a generation past slavery; [...] when someone like her couldn't vote for two reasons: because she was a woman and because of the color of her skin.

And tonight, I think about all that she's seen throughout her century in America – the heartache and the hope; the struggle and the progress; the times we were told that we can't, and the people who pressed on with that American creed: Yes we can.

At a time when women's voices were silenced and their hopes dismissed, she lived to see them stand up and speak out and reach for the ballot: Yes we can.

When there was despair in the Dust Bowl and Depression across the land, she saw a nation conquer fear itself with a New Deal, new jobs, a new sense of common purpose: Yes we can.

When the bombs fell on our harbor and tyranny threatened the world, she was there to witness a generation rise to greatness and democracy was saved: Yes we can.

She was there for the buses in Montgomery, the hoses in Birmingham, a bridge in Selma, and a preacher from Atlanta who told a people that "we shall overcome": Yes we can.

[...] And this year, in this election, she touched her finger to a screen, and cast her vote, because after 106 years in America, through the best of times and the darkest of hours, she knows how America can change: Yes we can.

Barack Obama, Election Day Speech, 4 November 2008.

CORRIGÉS

SE TESTER QUIZ

1 Traduire le lexique

1. a. annoyed: informal • b. pissed off: vulgar • c. discontented: formal

2. a. une bestiole inoubliable • b. admirer des peintures rupestres • c. des dossiers impossibles à obtenir

2 Utiliser les procédés de traduction

Les affirmations a et d sont vraies. L'affirmation b est fausse. La transposition induit un changement de catégorie grammaticale. L'affirmation c est fausse. C'est possible à l'aide de l'équivalence.

3 Résoudre les problèmes de traduction

1. Réponse b. *'s* après chaque prénom, donc ils ne sont pas frère et sœur. *Talk sb into + V-ing = convince sb to + BV.*

2. Réponse a. L'imparfait est induit par *and all the while* (= activité régulière).

3. Réponse b. Le *past perfect* n'a pas la même valeur dans les deux occurrences (situation qui perdure / élément déclencheur antérieur).

S'ENTRAÎNER

4 La transposition et la modulation

a. Il finit par entrer en titubant dans le canot de sauvetage. (transposition et modulation métonymique) • b. Ses ongles sont très négligés. (modulation assertive) • c. Une certaine Mme Jones n'arrête pas de téléphoner. (étoffement et modulation assertive) • d. Pense à ramener les enfants ! (modulation assertive)

5 L'équivalence

a. Il y a anguille sous roche. • b. Attention à la marche. • c. Ils se vendent comme des petits pains. • d. Ça coûte les yeux de la tête.

6 L'emploi des déterminants

a. Il promit la liberté à son esclave. • b. Elle s'est coupé le doigt alors qu'elle préparait le dîner. • c. Lorsque j'étais Ø enfant, je me déguisais en Ø pirate.

7 La voix passive et la voix active

1. Verbes à la voix passive : **was said to be, was offered, was turned into.**
Verbes à la voix active : **was, was learned, eluded, read.**

2. Elle était passionnée par la littérature anglaise. On disait d'elle qu'elle était un rat de bibliothèque et elle était en effet très savante. Seulement, la poésie romantique lui échappait jusqu'à ce qu'on lui offrit / offre les *Ballades lyriques* de Wordsworth. Elle les lut toutes rapidement et en fut ainsi changée en **romantique**.

CONSEIL
En français, les **adjectifs substantivés** qui se rapportent aux mouvements littéraires n'ont jamais de majuscule : les romantiques, les humanistes.

OBJECTIF BAC

8 Traduction en français

« Le problème, pour moi / à mon avis [rejeter le calque sur le français et opter pour une expression équivalente], c'est qu'on vous l'a dit [modulation pour traduire une structure passive + étoffement car « dire » appelle un complément] et pas dit / sans le dire. On vous l'a dit mais aucun d'entre vous ne comprend vraiment, et, j'ose le dire / l'affirmer, certains ne sont pas mécontents [modulation] de s'en tenir là [modulation]. Mais pas moi [transposition]. Si vous voulez / devez [*be going to* indique ici une intention] avoir une vie décente [au singulier] alors vous devez savoir et savoir vraiment / et comme il faut. Aucun d'entre vous n'ira en Amérique, aucun d'entre vous ne deviendra / sera star de cinéma. [...] Vos vies sont prédéfinies / toutes tracées [la structure passive et le choix lexical doivent respecter le caractère définitif de la formulation originelle]. Vous allez devenir des adultes, puis avant de devenir vieux, avant même d'atteindre la cinquantaine [équivalence], vous allez commencer à donner [choisir « donner » et pas « faire don de » qui suppose un consentement dont il n'est nullement question ici] vos organes vitaux. Voilà pour quoi on a créé chacun d'entre vous. [La traduction littérale, acceptable, omet l'empathie de la locutrice]. »

9 Transposition

Barack Obama, dans son discours de novembre 2008, présente sa victoire à l'élection présidentielle comme un événement inédit tout en l'inscrivant dans la continuité de l'histoire américaine. Aussi s'appuie-t-il sur l'anecdote d'une centenaire noire qui a voté pour balayer l'histoire des États-Unis depuis l'abolition de l'esclavage. Cela lui permet de dresser la liste des difficultés passées et surmontées par les Américains, mais surtout de prôner les valeurs communes et le progrès. Chaque référence à une évolution positive se conclut par la réaffirmation du rêve américain, synthétisé en une formule courte et inclusive : « Oui, nous le pouvons. » En suggérant que c'est pour cela que cette femme a voté pour lui, il associe sa victoire à la promesse d'une nouvelle ère de progrès.

9 Réussir l'épreuve orale

L'épreuve orale n'est pas une gageure : le dossier et le propos s'élaborent au fur et à mesure et l'aisance se construit au fil des entraînements.

35 Construire le dossier

En bref *À l'issue de deux années d'enseignement de la spécialité AMC vous serez évalué à l'écrit comme à l'oral. La partie orale s'appuie sur un dossier personnel que vous présenterez en anglais et dont la préparation requiert réflexion et minutie.*

I Composer le dossier

1 Personnaliser le dossier

- Vous devez constituer votre dossier (*set of documents*) de manière autonome, autour d'une **problématique** (*key question*).
- Pour ce faire, vous pouvez vous servir de documents étudiés en classe et ajouter des documents personnels trouvés lors de vos lectures et différentes recherches ou de vos sorties. Ce dossier est composé de 4 à 6 documents textuels et/ou iconographiques dont le fil conducteur se rattache à une ou plusieurs thématiques du programme du cycle terminal, c'est-à-dire « Savoirs, création, innovation », « Représentations » (1re), « Faire société », « Environnements en mutation » ou « Relation au monde » (Tle).

INFO
La **problématique** est la question posée en début de **présentation**, à laquelle vous devez répondre grâce à la mise en relation de vos différents documents.

2 Varier la nature des documents

Le dossier doit comprendre...

- au moins **1 article de presse**.
- au maximum **2 textes d'une autre nature** (discours, texte littéraire, essai, critique littéraire ou de cinéma, chanson, etc.).
- au maximum **2 documents iconographiques** (graphique, dessin de presse, affiche, photo, peinture, etc.).

II Assembler le dossier

1 Choisir les documents

■ Sélectionnez des documents qui illustrent la ou les thématique·s choisie·s et apportent des éléments complémentaires et / ou contradictoires pour répondre à votre problématique.

■ Ces documents doivent former un ensemble cohérent et riche, permettant de développer une argumentation dynamique qui s'appuie sur des va-et-vient constants entre ceux-ci.

2 Ordonner les documents

■ L'organisation du dossier et la définition de la problématique sont intimement liées. C'est en cherchant en quoi chaque document apporte un éclairage différent sur le·s thème·s du dossier que vous affinerez votre problématique. Celle-ci doit soulever un questionnement portant sur l'intégralité du dossier et non sur deux ou trois documents uniquement.

■ Les documents peuvent être agencés selon un ordre chronologique, diachronique ou thématique.

INFO

Ordre **chronologique** : du plus ancien au plus récent.
Ordre **diachronique** : suivant l'évolution des faits dans le temps.

zoom

Enrichir sa culture générale

Fréquenter régulièrement des sites anglophones vous permet à la fois d'améliorer votre anglais et d'enrichir votre culture générale.

■ **Chaînes d'information et journaux :**
→ BBC news – www.bbc.com/news
→ ABC news – abcnews.go.com
→ *The Guardian* – www.theguardian.com
→ *The New York Times* – www.nytimes.com

■ **Visites virtuelles de musées :**
→ Tate Modern – www.tate.org.uk
→ Guggenheim Museum – www.guggenheim.org
→ National Museum of African American History and Culture – nmaahc.si.edu

■ **Vidéos éducatives :**
→ Geography now – bit.ly/PbacAMC1re_35a
→ History – bit.ly/PbacAMC1re_35b
→ Every Frame A Painting.com (cinéma) – bit.ly/PbacAMC1re_35c

36 Présenter le dossier

En bref *La présentation orale du dossier requiert une préparation minutieuse pour répondre aux exigences de l'exercice et aux critères d'évaluation. Il faut bien comprendre ce que l'on attend de vous pour montrer votre maîtrise des attendus du programme de l'enseignement de spécialité pour le cycle terminal.*

I Comprendre les modalités de l'épreuve

1 Maîtriser le déroulé de l'épreuve

■ Il n'y a pas de temps de préparation. Vous donnerez un exemplaire du dossier à l'examinateur au début de votre prestation. Vous avez ensuite **dix minutes pour présenter votre dossier** sans intervention de l'examinateur.

■ Cette prise de parole en continu est suivie de **dix minutes d'échange** avec l'examinateur. La note maximale de 20/20 valide un niveau C1.

2 Prendre en compte les critères d'évaluation

Vous êtes évalué·e selon des critères précis dans **quatre domaines de compétence**.

Les 4 compétences évaluées

- **Richesse de la langue** : l'étendue de votre répertoire lexical incluant des expressions idiomatiques, des nuances de formulation et des structures variées et complexes.
- **Expression orale en continu** : votre capacité à présenter le dossier en développant une argumentation complexe et fluide à la fois, tout en vous assurant de sa réception.
- **Correction de la langue orale** : votre capacité à vous exprimer dans une langue correcte et fluide, avec une assez bonne maîtrise phonologique.
- **Interaction orale** : votre capacité à participer et construire l'échange tout en exploitant vos connaissances (inter)culturelles.

CONSEIL
Correction et richesse de la langue sont évaluées lors de la prise de parole en continu et de l'interaction, ne l'oubliez pas.

II Réussir la présentation orale

1 Respecter le temps imparti

- Vu le temps court dont vous disposez, il faut être synthétique. Donnez vos arguments et illustrez-les en faisant référence aux documents avec précision. Cela justifiera la constitution de votre dossier. L'introduction et la conclusion doivent respecter un timing strict : pas plus de deux minutes chacune.
- Vos références aux documents doivent être faites avec exactitude pour permettre à l'examinateur de vous suivre facilement.
- Pour favoriser la réception de votre présentation, il faut adopter une méthode claire et s'y conformer. Ainsi, avancer un argument et l'illustrer systématiquement par un exemple rend votre discours plus efficace.

2 Structurer la présentation

- Dans l'introduction, précisez la ou les thématique·s du dossier, présentez brièvement les **documents**, annoncez la problématique puis donnez le plan en une phrase maximum. Il s'agit de mettre en avant la logique interne du dossier.

> **CONSEIL**
> Pour respecter le timing sans précipitation, il vaut mieux donner peu d'information sur les **documents** et privilégier les trois autres points.

- Vous ne pourrez développer que trois points maximum, soulignant les échos entre les documents. Pour que l'on suive bien votre propos, il est primordial de marquer les différentes étapes (*To begin with / Firstly, Secondly, Thirdly...*).
- La conclusion doit être annoncée (*To conclude...*) et répondre à la problématique. Elle montre que les documents illustrent la thématique. Vous pouvez finir en inscrivant votre dossier dans l'actualité si cela s'y prête.

zoOm

Interpréter les questions lors de l'échange

Comprendre les questions permet d'y apporter des réponses adéquates.

Exemples de questions	Ce que l'on attend
Could you be specific about...? You mentioned... but it's slightly confusing; could you explain?	Préciser
What devices are used to show that...? Could you develop...?	Approfondir
Can you give instances of / another example of...? What elements show that...?	Illustrer
Don't you think that...? Can you qualify what you said about...?	Reconsidérer un choix

37 Améliorer sa prestation orale

En bref *Sans temps de préparation le jour J, l'épreuve orale suppose un entraînement rigoureux et régulier en amont. Vous devez faire une prestation fluide et maîtriser la phonologie anglaise.*

I S'entraîner à l'épreuve

1 Préparer la prise de parole

- Les dix premières minutes de votre présentation évalueront votre aptitude à vous **exprimer de manière fluide,** toute tentative d'apprendre par cœur et de réciter est à proscrire. Pour ce faire, vous devez vous entraîner régulièrement à prendre la parole à partir de vos notes afin de gagner en aisance.

- Pour **parler à partir de notes**, celles-ci doivent être visuelles et élaborées avec soin. Elles doivent reproduire votre plan à l'aide de mots-clés, de schémas, de chiffres, de dates et d'exemples. Ne rédigez pas vos phrases en intégralité. Vous pouvez ajouter des connecteurs logiques → FICHE 27 ou des **gap fillers** comme :

  Actually... Er... Well you see... Well, what I'm trying to say / to get at is... So my point is... Let me think... Anyway...

> **VOCABULARY**
> **Gap fillers** : mots ou expressions qui permettent de gagner du temps pour réfléchir lors d'une prise de parole.

2 Répéter dans les conditions réelles

- Lors de vos phases d'entraînement, il faut répéter votre discours à haute voix à l'aide de vos notes, et pourquoi pas vous filmer. En visionnant votre prestation vous pourrez vérifier si vous parvenez à adopter **un ton naturel, une expression fluide, une posture et un temps de parole convenables**.

- Faites une **courte pause** entre vos différentes parties, adoptez le **bon rythme** : ni trop rapide, ni trop lent, pour rester convaincant·e et éviter de faire une présentation monotone.

II Améliorer sa prononciation

> **INFO**
> Dans les transcriptions phonétiques, l'accent de mot est matérialisé par un petit trait vertical placé devant la **syllabe accentuée** : ˈ.

1 Bien prononcer et accentuer chaque mot

- Pour **vérifier la prononciation** d'un mot, il faut consulter sa transcription phonétique → RABATS dans un dictionnaire ou utiliser les sites qui permettent de l'écouter (wordreference.com, linguee.com). Il convient aussi de respecter l'accent de mot. Les mots anglais de deux syllabes ou plus ont toujours une **syllabe accentuée** : *dramatic* [drəˈmætɪk].

- Familiarisez-vous avec les règles de base.

• La plupart des noms ou adjectifs de deux syllabes sont accentués sur la première syllabe, alors que les verbes de deux syllabes sont accentués sur la seconde syllabe :

comfort (n), awful (adj), country (n) – return (v), depend (v), eject (v)

• Les mots terminés par *-ic, -tion, -sion, -cian* sont accentués sur l'avant-dernière syllabe :

information, discussion, musician, revision, economic

• Mais on compte aussi des irrégularités comme :

hotel, exam, happen, finish

2 | Respecter l'accent de phrase

- Vous devez respecter la musicalité de la langue pour produire des énoncés le plus authentique possible : intonation descendante dans les phrases déclaratives, montante dans les questions fermées (*yes-no questions*) et les énumérations.

- De plus, la succession des accents de mots donne le rythme de la phrase. L'accentuation étant une question de contrastes, certains mots sont prononcés de manière plus marquée que d'autres (*stressed and unstressed words*).

- Généralement les mots porteurs de sens sont accentués : noms, verbes, adjectifs qualificatifs, adverbes, mots interrogatifs, auxiliaires avec négation. Alors que les mots grammaticaux (articles, conjonctions, auxiliaires sans négation, déterminants possessifs, relatifs…) ne le sont pas.

zoOm

Gérer ses émotions

Un entraînement régulier permet d'aborder l'épreuve serein·e et confiant·e. Mais la prise de parole suscite souvent une forme d'appréhension.

Comment gérer son stress ?

Se préparer mentalement
L'épreuve n'est plus un saut dans l'inconnu. Visualisez le déroulé de votre prestation orale afin d'anticiper réactions et questions.

Rester positif•ive
Débarrassez-vous des pensées négatives : non, vous n'avez pas « tout oublié ». Souriez, le stress, raisonnable, est une énergie positive et développera votre confiance.

Éliminer les effets du stress
Respirez lentement et profondément pour libérer les tensions. N'allez pas trop vite, parlez clairement et suffisamment fort.

38 Être à l'aise à l'oral

En bref *Le fond de votre prestation doit prévaloir, mais vous devez également maîtriser votre voix, votre gestuelle et être capable de réagir avec à-propos.*

I Maîtriser la communication non verbale

1 Contrôler la gestuelle

- Votre message est véhiculé par votre corps tout entier. Évitez les gestes de fermeture comme par exemple les bras croisés. Adoptez une **posture ouverte et stable** : grandissez-vous.
- Adoptez une **gestuelle naturelle**. Que vous ayez tendance à parler avec les mains ou pas, il est important de rester fidèle à votre style personnel, mais restez sobre.

2 Contrôler le regard

- La communication passe aussi par le regard. Établissez tout de suite le **contact visuel** avec l'examinateur en le regardant dans les yeux. Ne fuyez pas son regard, même si vous êtes intimidé·e.
- Tout au long de votre prestation, vous devez **maintenir ce contact** avec l'examinateur. Mais sans le fixer de manière exagérée. Votre attitude ne doit pas créer une gêne ou une impression de défiance.

II Interagir avec l'examinateur

1 Entretenir un échange fluide

- Une fois votre présentation terminée, la phase d'interaction avec l'examinateur commence. Vous devez être à même de réagir rapidement et de manière adéquate en utilisant des expressions vous permettant de **maintenir et faire progresser l'interaction** avec l'examinateur.
- Si vous réalisez que l'examinateur perd le fil, n'hésitez pas à **reformuler ou expliquer** votre idée à l'aide d'exemples. À l'inverse, en cas d'incompréhension d'une question, soyez prêt·e à utiliser des expressions telles que :

  Would you mind repeating, please? Are you saying that...? What do you mean by...?

2 Savoir argumenter

- De manière générale, quelles que soient les idées exprimées, **soyez convaincant·e et justifiez** toujours vos propos. Mémorisez quelques structures permettant de rebondir sur un argument et d'exprimer l'accord ou le désaccord.

Structures pour…

reformuler
Actually… As a matter of fact… What I'm trying to get at is that…

exprimer votre point de vue personnel
To me… To my mind… It seems to me that… I believe that… I have the feeling that…

rebondir sur un argument
Yes, I suppose so. However… Well, in a way, but… That may be true but…

exprimer votre accord ou désaccord
Absolutely true! I totally agree with you… That's exactly what I think… I completely disagree with you… I really can't agree…

- Le **ton employé** rendra aussi votre propos convaincant, il faut parler d'une **voix claire et posée.** Respectez l'intonation des phrases, une voix monocorde devient vite ennuyeuse.

zoOm

Que faire de vos mains pendant que vous parlez ?

Évitez les gestes parasites qui risquent de détourner l'attention de l'examinateur.

✗ Jouer avec ses bijoux

✗ Se gratter ou tirer sur sa manche

✗ Jouer avec son stylo

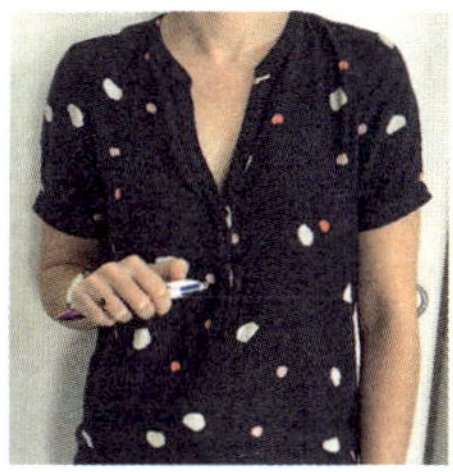

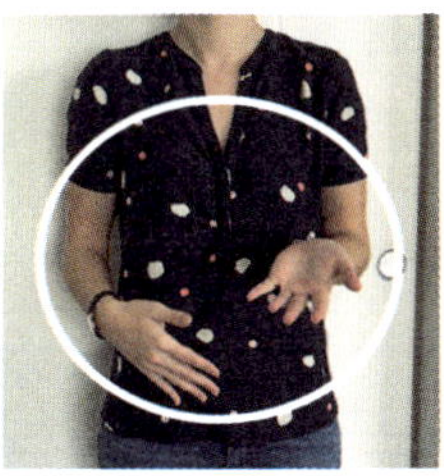

✔ Imaginer un cercle de cette taille et garder toujours ses mains à l'intérieur.

MÉMO VISUEL

1 Construire le dossier

Choisissez une ou plusieurs thématiques

- Prenez une thématique **qui vous parle**
- Faites-en le **fil conducteur** de votre dossier

Sélectionnez 4 à 6 documents

- **Variez** les types de documents
- Choisissez des documents qui **se complètent** et **se répondent**

Construisez votre dossier personnel

- Définissez une problématique qui prend en compte l'**intégralité** des documents
- **Ordonnez** les documents de façon cohérente

RÉUSSIR

4 Améliorer son expression orale

Gagnez en fluidité

- Entraînez-vous à parler **à partir de notes**
- Multipliez les **entraînements** et filmez-vous

Gagnez en authenticité

- Surveillez votre **débit** de parole
- Concentrez-vous sur l'**intonation** et la **prononciation**
- Ne négligez pas la **syntaxe**

L'ÉPREUVE ORALE

2 Présenter le dossier

Justifiez le choix des documents

- Montrez qu'ils **répondent** à votre problématique
- Montrez en quoi ils **illustrent** la ou les thématiques

Respectez le temps imparti

- Présentez une **argumentation** structurée et synthétique
- Faites une **introduction** succincte et consacrez davantage de temps aux arguments
- Ménagez des **transitions** claires

3 Être à l'aise à l'oral

Favorisez la communication

- Adoptez une **posture** ouverte et stable
- Évitez toute **attitude** de repli sur soi
- Canalisez votre **stress**

Interagissez efficacement

- Anticipez les **questions**
- Utilisez des **expressions clés**
- **Reformulez** votre propos

Maintenez l'attention du correcteur

- Accrochez le **regard** de l'interlocuteur
- Soyez **convaincant·e**
- Parlez d'une **voix** claire et posée

S'ENTRAÎNER

Pour l'épreuve orale du bac, vous composez votre dossier en choisissant des documents qui vous ont plu, interpellé·e, intéressé·e ou choqué·e. Ici, nous vous proposons de vous entraîner sur un dossier de 5 documents.
Ce dossier s'appuie sur la thématique « Savoirs, création, innovation », et plus précisément sur l'axe « Sciences et techniques, promesses et défis ». Les 5 documents sont un communiqué de presse, un extrait de nouvelle, un graphique, un article de presse et un dessin humoristique.

1 Exploiter le dossier

1. Observez et lisez les 5 documents proposés.

Document A At UN, robot Sophia joins meeting on artificial intelligence and sustainable development

Artificial intelligence has the potential to accelerate progress on global development goals, but also poses a range of complex challenges, including ethical questions, human rights issues and security risks, speakers told a United Nations event today that featured a robot as one of the panellists.

A moment that drew big applause during the day-long event, "The future of everything – sustainable development in the age of rapid technological change," came when Sophia, a humanoid robot, had brief interaction with UN Deputy Secretary-General Amina J. Mohammed.

To Ms. Mohammed's question about what the UN can do to help people in many parts of the world who have no access to the Internet or electricity, Sophia said "the future is already here. It's just not very evenly distributed [...]," quoting renowned science fiction writer William Gibson. "If we are smarter and focused on win-win type of results, A.I. [artificial intelligence] could help proficiently distribute the world's existing resources like food and energy."

Sophia is Hanson Robotics' latest and most advanced robot. Sophia has also become a media sensation, having given numerous interviews to multiple media outlets, performed in concert, and even graced the cover of one of the top fashion magazines

In her opening speech, Ms. Mohammed warned that despite profound potential for accelerating progress on the Sustainable Development Goals (SDGs), if technological progress is not managed well, it risks exacerbating existing inequalities.

"The influence of technology on our societies should be determined by the actions of us, humans, not by machines," she said. "Technology is here for us to explore and use for the benefit of all."

Document B

In a post-apocalyptic future humans create computers to fight their wars. Computers join together into one unified computer, AM, which becomes conscious.

The Cold War started and became World War Three and just kept going. It became a big war, a very complex war, so they needed the computers to handle it. They sank the first shafts and began building AM[1]. There was the Chinese AM and the Russian AM and the Yankee AM [...]. But one day AM woke up and knew who he was, and he linked himself, and he began feeding all the killing data, until everyone was dead, except for the five of us. [...]

We had given AM sentience[2].

Harlan Ellison, *I Have No Mouth, and I Must Scream*, 1967,
© Estate Harlan Ellison, D.R.

1. AM (Allied Mastercomputer) is the main antagonist of the short story.
2. sentience: consciousness

Document C Service robots for professional use

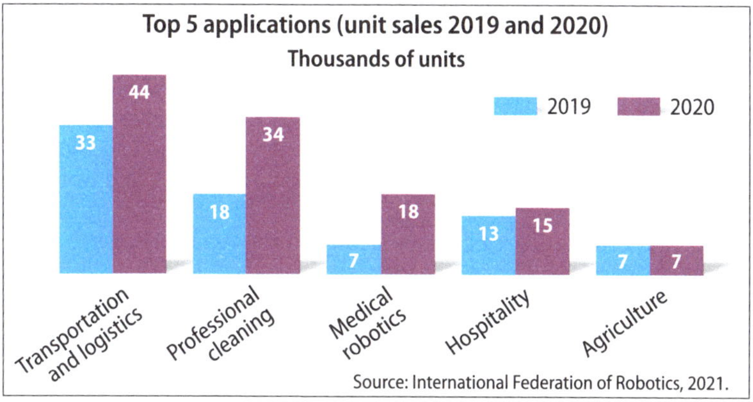

INFO

A **service robot** is a semi-autonomous or fully autonomous robot that has some mobility and can interact with people (retail, hospitality = hotel industry, healthcare, warehouse, space and defense, agricultural applications, and police work). Some can have a humanoid form.

Document D AI will be able to beat us at everything by 2060, say experts

Enjoy beating robots while you still can. There is a 50 per cent chance that machines will outperform humans in all tasks within 45 years, according to a survey of more than 350 artificial intelligence researchers.

AI will master many activities a lot sooner, though. Machines are predicted to be better than us at translating languages by 2024, writing high-school essays by 2026, driving a truck by 2027, working in retail by 2031, writing a bestselling book by 2049 and surgery by 2053. In fact, all human jobs will be automated within the next 120 years, say respondents.

The survey, by the University of Oxford and Yale University, was sent to AI researchers who published in 2015 at one of two big conferences in the field – the Conference on Neural Information Processing Systems and the International Conference on Machine Learning. In total, 352 people responded. [...]

But at least we will still be around to deal with these issues. Despite media hype about the dangers of AI, the researchers put only a 5 per cent chance on computers bringing about outcomes near the level of human extinction.

One-trick AI

AIs can already outperform humans in many tasks. AlphaGo, Google DeepMind's AI, has just beaten the best human Go player in the world. Other systems can lip-read better than professionals or help detectives sift through police data. Yet each of these is only good at one task and would be useless at most others unless retrained.

"There is accumulating evidence that machines can overpower human intelligence in complex, though specific tasks," says Eleni Vasilaki at the University of Sheffield in the UK. But there is little evidence that AI with human-like versatility will appear any time soon, she says.

Timothy Revell, *New Scientist*, 31 May 2017.

Document E

"The good news, Dave, is that the computer's passed the Turing test. The bad news is that you've failed."

Chris Madden, *Turing test*.

INFO

British mathematician Alan Turing invented a test to determine whether a computer can think like a human being or not. The **Turing test** consists of a human interrogator exchanging written messages with an unknown partner to find out if this is a human or a machine.

2. Complétez le tableau suivant en listant les idées principales de chaque document, en lien avec le thème proposé.

Doc	Type de document	Idées principales
A		• .... • .... • ....
B		• .... • .... • ....
C		• .... • .... • ....
D		• .... • .... • ....
E		• .... • .... • ....

2 Trouver une problématique

Une problématique est intéressante et pertinente lorsqu'elle fait réfléchir. Pour cela, il faut essayer d'y intégrer deux éléments conflictuels.

1. a) Dégagez 2 ou 3 grands thèmes opposés en surlignant, à l'aide d'un code couleur, les idées extraites des documents (cf. tableau de l'exercice précédent).

b) Résumez chaque thème en une ligne.

- Thème 1 : ....
- Thème 2 : ....
- Thème 3 : ....

2. Complétez les amorces de phrases suivantes pour formuler une problématique que les thèmes dégagés pourraient illustrer.

(To what extend) can .... ?
Should there be limits to............ ?

CONSEIL
Les thèmes que vous dégagez des documents vous aident à construire et à préciser votre problématique. Vous pourrez alors changer certains documents selon le point de vue que vous souhaitez illustrer.

3 Construire le plan

1. Ordonnez vos idées en 2 ou 3 parties. À partir de la problématique choisie, comment organiseriez-vous les parties ?

• Partie I : ....
• Partie II : ....
• (Partie III : ....)
• Conclusion : ....
....

CONSEIL
Vous êtes libre d'organiser vos parties comme vous le souhaitez : en développant un point positif puis en soulignant qu'il y a aussi des points négatifs, ou au contraire en allant du négatif au positif.

2. Dans votre développement, vous ne présenterez pas les documents un à un mais vous tirerez de chacun d'entre eux les éléments nécessaires à votre démonstration, au déroulement de votre présentation. Quel ordre donneriez-vous aux 5 documents afin de mettre en valeur vos idées ?

OBJECTIF BAC

4 Mettre en relation les documents et préparer sa présentation

1. Complétez la trame de votre plan à l'aide de mots clés et d'exemples tirés des documents sur lesquels vous vous appuyez pour expliquer vos idées. Vous n'avez pas à utiliser tous les documents à chaque fois.

Votre brouillon peut prendre la forme d'un tableau de ce type :

Partie I	
Partie II	
(Partie III)	
Conclusion	

2. Utilisez les conseils → FICHE 36 pour rédiger introduction et conclusion.

5 Préparer l'entretien

Après votre présentation orale, vous devrez répondre aux questions du jury. Anticiper ces questions vous permettra de mieux vous y préparer.

Que répondriez-vous à ces trois questions types du jury ?

1. Why have you chosen this axis?
2. Can you justify the order of the documents you have presented?
3. Is this topic being currently debated in the news?

CORRIGÉS

S'ENTRAÎNER

1 Exploiter le dossier

1. et 2.

Doc	Type	Idées principales
A	Press release from the United Nations	• Robotics accelerates progress • Challenges: ethical questions, human rights, security risks • AI can help distribute natural ressources to countries in need • Sophia humanoid: concerts / interviews / fashion magazine / invited at the UN • "The influence of technology on our societies should be determined by the actions of humans, not by machines"
B	Extract from a short story	• Humans created a supercomputer (AM) to win WW3 • AM becomes more intelligent than humans and kills all human beings but 5 • Machines overpowering men
C	Graph	• A service robot can move and interact with people / it is an assistant • Huge increase in the worldwide sales of cleaning, medical, logistics and transportation robots • Smaller increase in agriculture and hospitality
D	Press article	• Machines will outperform humans in any tasks within 45 years • AI so good it is difficult to distinguish what AI does and what human beings do • Scientists say the human race won't be destroyed • AI can excel at some specific tasks but not versatile / polyvalent / AI can only do what it is trained for
E	Cartoon	• The Turing test can help decide if a machine can think as a human being • The machine passes the test / the human being fails: machines superior to humans

2 Trouver une problématique

1. Les idées extraites des documents peuvent être regroupées en trois grands thèmes :
- Thème 1 : the development of AI and robots helps improve our lives
- Thème 2 : but there are risks and challenges
- Thème 3 : scientists confirm AI is not a danger so there shouldn't be any limits to improving AI

2. La problématique pourrait être la suivante :
(To what extent) can AI and robots threaten our society?
Should there be limits to the development of AI and robots?

3 Construire le plan

1. Voici une proposition de plan :
- Partie I : Fascination for robots & AI
- Partie II : But also fear of robots & AI
- Conclusion : Scientists confirm AI can be trusted / humanity is not threatened / no need for limits if humans stay in charge

2. D'après ce plan, les documents seraient présentés dans l'ordre suivant : A – C – B – E – D.

OBJECTIF BAC

4 Mettre en relation les documents et préparer sa présentation

1. *Ce tableau propose une trame de votre présentation au brouillon.*

Partie I **Fascination**	• Source of fascination: doc A (Sophia = superstar → TV, fashion magazine, UN) • At the core of progress: doc A (Sophia) + doc C (service robots in different fields) • Help distribute ressources (doc A) • Supercomputers help winning a war: doc B (like **Alan Turing's "Bombe"** decoding machine which helped decypher the Nazi codes during WW2)
Partie II **Fear = risks**	• Security risks like hacking: doc A • Machines outperforming humans: doc D + E • Loss of jobs which become automated: doc D • Machines overpowering men and destroying humanity: doc B
Conclusion	AI is superintelligent but not versatile: can only do what it has been taught (doc D) AI is not a threat: doc A Challenge = men need to stay in charge: doc A

CONSEIL
L'ajout de **références culturelles personnelles** enrichira votre présentation.

2. *Voici une proposition d'introduction et de conclusion.*

Introduction

Science is part of our lives. It's been evolving tremendously for the past decades, reaching levels of technology that couldn't have been foreseen. Artificial intelligence and robots are everywhere, from industry 4.0 to medicine, domotics and transportation. Be it in fiction or reality, some people have always feared artificial intelligence, saying it could destroy humanity. We can wonder to what extend there should be limits to this double-edged tool. First we will present the fascination around artificial intelligence. In a second part we will explain why it can also be feared.

Conclusion

Possibilities offered by artificial intelligence seem endless. It makes our lives easier, safer and more entertaining. But even if fiction has often spread anxiousness through many films, we can trust scientists when they say humanity isn't threatened. No need for limits to be set as long as humans stay in charge, acting positively. Indeed ethics must remain at the core of any scientific research. That's why transhumanism, which prones eternal digital life, may be our next threat.

5 Préparer l'entretien

1. I've chosen this axis because I've always been interested in science and its innovations. Science is part of our everyday lives. It's important to question its limits.
2. The documents follow the outline of my presentation. In my first part I've focused on the positive impact of AI and robots so I wanted to illustrate this with documents which depict a positive vision of science. Then I have insisted on the negative side with the cartoon and the short story which portray a frightening vision of technology. The final document states the scientists' opinion which is really reassuring.
3. Science touches every single field of our lives. Let's take the example of Elon Musk who is a billionaire entrepreneur who tackles so many science domains from AI to space and medicine.

CONSEIL

Renseignez-vous sur les personnes clés du dossier (auteurs, personnalités, scientifiques), soyez capable de définir les éléments clés (*AI*, *robotics*, *humanoids*), enrichissez vos références culturelles sur la thématique (*Hanson Robotics*, *Turing test*...), suivez l'actualité liée à ce sujet tout au long de l'année.

CRÉDITS PHOTOGRAPHIQUES

4 H	ph © Getty Images/iStockphoto
4 B	ph © Bettmann Archive/Getty Images
5	ph © «Black Panther», 2018, de Ryan Coogler based on the comics characters created by Jack Kirby & Stan Lee, Coll. Christophel © Marvel Studios - Walt Disney Pictures
6 H	Stéphane Mattern
6 B	Stéphane Mattern
7	ph © Getty Images/iStockphoto
11	capture d'écran © IBM - Digital Nation Africa, 4/02/021
13	capture d'écran © TED
15	capture d'écran © 2022 Khan Academy
16	ph © Photo12/Alamy/World Archive
17	ph © Getty Images/iStockphoto
29	ph © Photo12/Alamy/Ascannio
31	ph © Photo12/Alamy/World Archive
33	ph © «I robot» 2004 Real Alex Proyas. Coll. Christophel © DavisEntertainment/Laurence Mark Productions
37	ph © Photo12/Alamy/Ascannio
39	ph © Bloomberg/Getty Images
41	© Drew Panckeri/cartoonstock.com
51	ph © Bettmann Archive/Getty Images
53	ph © Photo12/Alamy/Artefact
57	ph © Bettmann Archive/Getty Images
59	ph © Win McNamee/Getty Images/AFP
61	ph © Santi Visalli/Getty Images
73	ph © Stuart Miles - stock.adobe.com
79	ph © Coll. Christophel © Amblin Entertainment - DreamWorks - Pascal Pictures – Star Thrower Entertainment
83	ph © Frank Augstein/AP/SIPA
85	© Victor Ndula/Cartoon Movement
95	ph © «Black Panther» 2018, de Ryan Coogler based on the comics characters created by Jack Kirby & Stan Lee, Coll. Christophel © Marvel Studios - Walt Disney Pictures
97	ph © Cylla von Tiedemann
99	ph © Ryan M. Kelly/AFP
101	ph © Cecil Beaton/Camerapress/Gamma
103	ph © «Black Panther» 2018, de Ryan Coogler based on the comics characters created by Jack Kirby & Stan Lee. Coll. Christophel © Marvel Studios - Walt Disney Pictures
104	ph © Photo12/Alamy/Yaacov Dagan
105	ph © Thananit - stock.adobe.com
107	© John W. Mills, photo : Photo12/Alamy/World History Archive
117, 128	© Stéphane Mattern
123	ph © Tierney - stock.adobe.com
128, 129	ph © rashadashurov - stock.adobe.com, Happy Art - stock.adobe.com, tomes1985 – stock.adobe.com
134	ph © Steve Espo Powers, photo Vanessa Carvalho/Brazil Photo Press /AFP
139, 149	© Stéphane Mattern
148, 149	ph © rashadashurov - stock.adobe.com, Happy Art - stock.adobe.com, tomes1985 – stock.adobe.com
155, 166	© Stéphane Mattern
166, 167	ph © rashadashurov - stock.adobe.com, Happy Art - stock.adobe.com, tomes1985 – stock.adobe.com
173, 183	© Stéphane Mattern
182, 183	ph © rashadashurov - stock.adobe.com, Happy Art - stock.adobe.com, tomes1985 – stock.adobe.com
186	© Chris Madden

PAPIER À BASE DE FIBRES CERTIFIÉES

Hatier s'engage pour l'environnement en réduisant l'empreinte carbone de ses livres. Celle de cet exemplaire est de :
500 g éq. CO_2
Rendez-vous sur www.hatier-durable.fr

Achevé d'imprimer en Italie par L.E.G.O. S.p.A. - Lavis (TN)
Dépôt légal : 08675-3/01 - Juin 2022